T0041596

Section 130

By
Katrinka Mannelly

ZMOK
BOOKS

SECTION 130
By Katrinka Mannelly
Cover design by Vincent Rospond
This edition published in 2019

Zmok Books, is an imprint of

Pike and Powder Publishing Group LLC

1525 Hulse Rd, Unit 1   1 Craven Lane, Box 66066
Point Pleasant, NJ 08742   Lawrence, NJ 08648-66066

Copyright © Katrinka Mannelly
ISBN 978-1-945430-76-3
LCN 2019936133

Bibliographical References and Index
1. Fiction. 2. Horror. 3. Dark Fantasy

Pike and Powder Publishing Group LLC All rights reserved
For more information on Pike and Powder Publishing Group, LLC,
visit us at www.PikeandPowder.com & www.wingedhussarpublishing.com

twitter: @pike_powder
facebook: @PikeandPowder

This book is sold subject to the condition that it shall not, by way of trade or otherwise, be lent, resold, hired out, or otherwise circulated without the publisher's prior consent in any form of binding or cover other than that in which it is published and without a similar condition, including this condition, being imposed on the subsequent purchaser.

The scanning, uploading, and distribution of this book via the Internet or via any other means without the permission of the publisher is illegal and punishable by law. Please purchase only authorized electronic editions, and do not participate in or encourage electronic piracy of copyrighted materials. Your support of the author's and publisher's rights is appreciated. Karma, it's everywhere.

Like every important thing I do, this book is dedicated to my husband Brian and daughter Tigist.

Section 130

by

Katrinka Mannelly

Stories

Snap...2

Makes Perfect Sense....................................16

Flap...25

The Smile She Deserved.............................34

Hardly Any Feel Left....................................42

Believe...52

More Annoying Than Burs in the Fur.................60

Tooth Exchange International Consultants.........71

The Twenty-Seventh Try.............................87

You All Leave...102

Offending the Senses...................................113

Safe, Welcome, and Included...................129

Resurrecting Rocky......................................144

Under the Folds of A Homemade Flag.................154

A Tempting Transaction.............................164

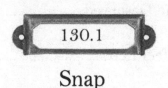

Snap

The knock startled Eleanor. Nobody knocked on the door of a third floor walkup. 'I probably shouldn't answer' flashed through her mind as she opened it.

A lanky teenage girl looked at Eleanor, sighed, and brushed past her into the apartment. She smelled like a wood-burning stove.

"Excuse me. You can't just walk in here. Who are you?"

"I don't excuse you. I just did. And I'm Jezebeth." With that, the scruffy teen plopped down on the couch.

"Do I know you?"

"Nope."

"Are you here for Viv or Denise? Because they're not here."

"No. I guess I should have said, 'you don't

know me yet.' I'm here for you, E. I chose a time I knew your roommates would be away for a while."

"My name is Eleanor, not E, and nobody calls me that anyway. How do you know about my roommates? Don't sit on my couch. You smell weird. Either tell me who you are, or get out."

"I told you. I'm Jezebeth, and I'm calling you E from here on."

"Are you on drugs?"

"No. Do you have any? 'Cuz, E, that would be awesome."

"I don't take drugs."

"I didn't think so. I'm a demon from hell. You sent for me, E."

"Excuse me?"

"I all ready told you, I don't excuse you, so stop asking."

"I didn't send for any demon from hell. You need to get out now, or I'll call the police."

"Go ahead and call. It'll just delay things, and I'm in no hurry. Plus, I have lots of tricks. You will get all frustrated and flustered when they get here and I'll enjoy it quite a bit. I believe the number is 911?"

This tall, tanned, dark-haired teen in frayed black clothes looked more like an undernourished punk rocker wannabe than a demon.

"Okay, I'm guessing this is a prank. It's not working."

"You don't have any friends who would prank you. Actually, you don't really have that many friends at all, do you, E?"

That hit a nerve. It was one of many sore subjects for Eleanor, who unconsciously crossed her arms and tightened her jaw, "Okay, tell me this, Demon Girl, when exactly did I send for you?"

"You exactly sent for me, E, when you were at the club Avenue C with people from work – who aren't really your friends, FYI – Jason the temp went to the bathroom and you said, 'I'd let the devil do his worst for one night with that temp.'"

Eleanor blushed all over her small, pale body. Bombed out of her mind on Riesling and daiquiris, she had said that, and she regretted it.

"Do you know Jason? Are you his under-aged girlfriend or something? Because it was barely even a one night stand, and it was almost a month ago."

"Oh, I know. And no, I don't know Jason except what I read about him in your file. I told you, I'm a demon, and by the way, I'm older than I look. About the timing, I have a huge caseload and things are always backed up in Hell."

"I have a file in Hell?"

"Yep. You started it when you proffered the deal. The phrase we really like to hear is 'I'd sell my soul for…,' but you went with the softball, 'I'd let the devil do his worst for…' and I'm his worst, which actually means I'm the best at what I do, and I'm here to torment you per your deal."

"You are here to torment me?"

"Yep. When it comes to me, that's what 'his worst' means."

"So how are you going to do it?"

"We'll see." With that Jezebeth picked up one of Viv's People magazines and started flipping through the pages with the quick rhythm of a metronome, obviously uninterested.

"Are you doing that to annoy me?"

"Does it annoy you?"

"No," Eleanor snapped, even though it did, a lot. She sat across from Jezebeth in an over-stuffed chair feeling uncomfortably out of control and trying to figure out her next move. The room went silent except for the steady sound of page flipping.

"Prove you're a demon."

"Why?"

"You've given me no reason to believe you're a demon, so prove it."

"Ask nicely."

"What?"

"Ask nicely."

Eleanor did not want to ask nicely, but she didn't want to back down either. Through gritted teeth, Eleanor said, "Please prove it" in the most sarcastic tone she could muster.

Jezebeth pulled off her shabby knit beanie, and parted her hair so two small horns showed through. They were short, about two inches, blood red, and looked like bone.

"Wanna see my tail too?"

Eleanor tried to hide her shock. Jezebeth slid her beanie back on and gloated. She leaned back, laced her hands behind her head, and crossed her feet on the coffee table.

"Denise is very particular about that table. Get your boots off it."

Eleanor yanked the table about six inches in her direction, leaving Jezebeth's feet unsupported. They stuck out suspended for a minute until Jezebeth lowered them. Then she leaned forward, stared Eleanor in the eyes, placed the tips of all ten fingernails on the table, and slowly scraped her hands back. A painful screech filled Eleanor's ears, and the stink of burnt lacquer assaulted her nose as ten long scratches materialized on the table.

"That was unprofessional. In fact, you're fired. Get out."

Jezebeth laughed. "You can't fire me, E."

"Why not? I'm your client, and I am unhappy with your service. That's how it works. You're fired."

"You are not my client. You're my victim, my assignment, my case. You don't get to call the shots."

"Then I want to speak to your boss."

"You want to speak to Satan?"

"Yes. I'd like to register a complaint. You said you are the best at this, and clearly you're not."

"You want to complain to Satan that I'm not good enough at tormenting you?"

"He should be aware that his so called 'best demon' sucks at her job."

"How so, E?"

"For one thing, my name's not E. In addition, you haven't explained anything to me. I don't know the schedule. When do you intend to start or stop? What kind of torment you will be employing? You seem to have no process. I personally live by Blain Gold's Three P's of Management. Surely you've heard of it? I mean, do you even have a plan? Procedures you follow or anything? All you've done so far is pretend to read a magazine and destroy my roommate's property."

"Wow. You're a piece of work. Your file says you're a tight-ass, but you take the cake, E."

"My file does not say I'm a tight-ass. I'm not a tight-ass."

"You are and it does, E."

"I am an organized, confident, competent woman. Unlike you, I am good at my job."

"You are an uptight, bossy, pain-in-the-ass, and I guess that makes you an adequate event planner at the Family Fun-Time Inn, but that's not much to write home about, E. The truth is, they tolerate you at the office because you are so controlling you do all the work, and everyone else gets to slide by. It's all in your file."

Another direct hit and it stung, but Eleanor was not one to concede. "I think what you mean is, I'm smart. Being indispensable at work is smart."

"So you're a smart cookie, E? You, who traded torment for a night with Jason the temp? Tell me E, how'd that work out for you?"

Horrible. Jason had given new meaning the to term 'selfish lover.' Eleanor woke up the next morning alone under a comforter crusted in puke, completely unsatisfied, with thirty bucks missing off her dresser. But instead of going into any of that, Eleanor changed the subject. "Do you intend to inflict pain? I have a high tolerance, but my teeth are off limits. My parents paid a lot for orthodontia. I'm thinking we should get started soon. I have a big day tomorrow. I have very large family reunion group coming in to tour the space, so I'd really like to get this over with."

"Hey, E? I don't tell you how to do your stupid job, so don't tell me how to do mine." Jezebeth picked up another of Viv's endless supply of People magazines and went back to disinterested flipping.

Eleanor couldn't stand it. "You suck. I'm going to bed."

After about ninety minutes Eleanor came back into the living room in a matching pajama and robe set. "I can't sleep. I keep thinking you're going to spring into my bedroom with an air horn or a bucket of cold water or something."

Jezebeth did not look up from her latest magazine. "That's an insult, E. An air horn? I'm no amateur."

"Well, you're no pro either. Do you realize you've been here for hours and you've done nothing? The waiting is maddening, so could you please get on with it all ready? Do you remember that I mentioned Blain Gold's Three P's of Management? Blain teaches that planning, productivity, and process equal progress."

"Isn't that four Ps?"

"That's a common misunderstanding of those who have not actually attended the seminars; the three Ps of management result in the ultimate P, success. It is a great system and Blain's a genius. I consider him a mentor really. Even though we've only met in person for a few minutes during a Q and A session, we connect he and I. I can bring you a few of his books if you want to take a look."

Jezebeth continued flipping.

Eleanor tried another tack, "Jezebeth, I'm not sure if you're inept — perhaps due to lack of training, or lazy, or uninspired, but nothing is happening here, so I was thinking, maybe you have an evaluation of some sort? Like a Survey Monkey? I could fill it out and say you did a great job tormenting me, even though you haven't. I could swear you were here all night torturing away while really you could go anywhere and do anything you want. Find somebody with drugs, since you're into that. It could be a win-win. You get a free night out, and I get to put this whole thing behind me and get some sleep. What do you think?"

"Nice try, E, but no."

Exasperated, Eleanor looked around and noticed something she hadn't before on the table. "Is that Donny's water? Did you get that from my fridge? Did you drink it?"

"Yeah. I got thirsty and found this bottle. Oh, I also ate the leftover spaghetti and a box of Thin Mints I found in the freezer. What's the big deal, E?"

"I can't believe it. You drank Donny's water. That is a bottle that Donny Osmond drank from. Do you not see how it says 'Donny's water' in big, black, sharpie letters? Jeez! I snatched it at a book signing he did. I've had that for six years. It is one of my most prized possessions, and you drank it. That's it. That. Is. It. We're done here. You are the worst demon ever. You drank Donny's water. And you ate my lunch for tomorrow and Viv planned for those cookies to last her a year — that's why they were in the freezer. Get out."

"Okay, I can see getting upset about the lunch and the cookies, but six-year-old backwash from a B-lister is just sad. And gross. I can't believe I drank it. Yuck."

"You stole from me. Get. Out."

"I'm a demon, E. We steal stuff all the time so…sorry, not sorry. And like I keep telling you,

I'll decide when we're done here."

Eleanor fumed, marched back to her bedroom, and hollered, "I hate you. You owe me a celebrity water, and lunch, and cookies, and a new table too." She slammed the door behind her.

Jezebeth kept flipping.

Around 6 a.m. a beaten, exhausted version of Eleanor reappeared. Jezebeth understood the look well. She knew Eleanor had imagined a thousand different horrors that night. Knew she had lamented at least a hundred ways that her life was less meaningful and special without her precious Donny water. And knew she had turned over and over in her mind everything Jezebeth was doing wrong. Eleanor's eyes looked glazed over and her whole faced was puffed from lack of sleep and crying. Her shoulders slumped in defeat. "Um, I wrote that complaint memo, to your boss that we talked about." Eleanor weakly held up a note.

Jezebeth stood and took it from her. "Damn E, you didn't just ruminate, you wrote it down and addressed it to Satan himself. The tight-asses should make you their queen."

On Hello Kitty stationary in neat penmanship it said:

MEMO

TO: Satan, Lucifer (Morning Star), Beelzebub, Devil, Prince of Power, et al.

RE: Jezebeth

Satan,

As you know, on the evening of Thursday, March 14, 2017, one demon Jezebeth was dispatched from Hell to torment one Eleanor Rose Hitchcock (me). I regret to inform you she has not fulfilled her duties, and her services have been poor, if not extremely unprofessional. See the bullets below:

•   If she had done her research she would know that it is well established that I am afraid of: clowns, earwigs, ankle fat, The Blair Witch Project, and the dark. Jezebeth does not seem to know this, has not so much as mentioned any of these, nor has she even attempted to turn off the lights (such a simple, obvious tactic).

•   There has been no physical injury, or even threat of injury to my person.

•   She did irreparable damage to one of my roommate's tables and ate an entire box of my other roommate's Thin Mint cookies. As neither of these women were her assigned client, I expect you or she will make restitution for these items. Note: the table was a gift purchased in Thailand and the cookies, sold by the Girl Scouts of America, are only available for a limited time, so your procurement department should get to work on replacing these items A.S.A.P. (as soon as possible).

• *No attempt whatsoever has been made to explain any plan of action for torment. I have no idea what to expect and no vision of what she intends. Nor has a timetable been discussed.*

• *She also called me a "tight-ass" which is extremely inappropriate and untrue. I am a smart, organized, confident, competent woman. There is a big difference between the two.*

• *Overall, I rate Jezebeth's performance as exceedingly unsatisfactory.*

In conclusion, I am surprised that an authority such as yourself would not utilize a quality management system. I strongly recommend Blain Gold's Three P's of Management. Your demon, Jezebeth, would most certainly benefit from Blain's proven system and training. Please contact me by cell phone at 286.444.9021 with questions or to discuss any of this in greater detail.

Jezebeth examined messy, tired, broken Eleanor. "Wow, E. I kind of admire you. You have tenacity, and that's something I really believe in. But you are also coo-coo for coco puffs." Jezebeth ripped up the memo.

Eleanor didn't have much left. She sort of flopped her head around, spread out her hands, and whined, "What's wrong with you? Why are you dragging this out? What did you even do all night?"

Jezebeth dropped back down on the couch. "You know. This."

Snap.

Jezebeth didn't hear it. She felt it. It reverberated through the room and made her bones hum.

"This? Well, I can't stand this! This sucks and you suck! Please just torment me! Do it now! Get it over with! This is torture! You are the worst! I hate this and I hate you! Torment me all ready, you jerk!"

Ah, the true breaking point, sweet, sweet music to Jezebeth's ears. Less than twenty-four hours, too. She grinned. I've still got it. "Told you, E. I'm his worst, which means I'm the best, the best at what I do."

Makes Perfect Sense

With great anticipation, Tam prepared to meet her spirit animal.

In her trance-like meditative state she saw herself, in her mind's eye, walking across a small wooden bridge toward her imagined safe and sacred space. For Tam, this meant a sunny meadow filled with yellow and white wildflowers that swayed together in the breeze. As directed by Coco, the facilitator, Tam looked down toward her feet.

Then Coco prompted Tam and the rest of the group to look up slowly. Tam inhaled, excited and eager. She gazed out at...what the hell? Tam shook her head side to side. No. No, no, no, no!

The workshop attendees organized themselves into a loose circle on the laminate wood floor of the church basement meeting room. They sat on folded Mexican blankets. Tall bookshelves around the perimeter of the room hadn't bothered Tam before, but now they loomed, making her feel surrounded. The warm smell of the sage Coco burned to purify the room still lingered. Tam knew the fragrance should relax her, but at the moment she found it annoying.

"Let's go around the group and share what we saw," Coco said. "Brittney, we'll start with you."

Brittney was Tam's crazy, dreadlocked, colorful, barista friend. She had talked Tam into signing up for the session.

"It was so amazing, Coco. I saw a monarch butterfly."

"Did that make sense to you?"

"It did. It did." Brittney nodded. "I'm a traveler and butterflies have wings, they migrate. I'm hoping to see the whole world some day. It's just so perfect for me." She was still nodding.

"They're beautiful too, just like you, Brittney. How totally spot-on," Coco added. "Tam, how about you?"

"Pass."

"Pass? No, Tam you can't pass. You did see an animal didn't you?"

Tam wished she could lie like other people, but her stepfather could never abide lying, so he had raised it right out of Tam and her sister.

"Yes." Tam squirmed.

"This is a circle of safety, Tam. You're among friends. If you tell us what you saw, we can help you understand it. It can sometimes be hard for people. Men sometimes see what they interpret as a feminine animal like a cat or women see a masculine animal like a bear. Sometimes people see an animal that has been vilified by our culture, like a snake. It can be confusing, but if you share with us, we can help you figure it out."

Being a Vietnamese woman in America, Tam was used to being patronized. God knows it happened all day at the nail salon where she worked, so she quickly jumped to this conclusion.

"Do people often get confused by seeing a chicken?" She snapped.

Coco paused a beat before responding. "Is it a proud Bantam or crowing rooster?"

"No. It's a plain white chicken. Like a fryer."

After another tick of silence Coco said, "Tam, you are special. You must be quite unique. I've never had a chicken before in any of my groups."

Tam supposed Coco kept this response in her back pocket, reserved for the real duds, when there was nothing else to say.

They continued through the rest of the group and heard about an otter, a gazelle, a hawk, and a cougar – all respectable totems.

Tam berated herself the whole way as she walked home. How had she let Brittney talk her into this? Over a week's coffee orders they discussed the workshop. By the second or third day Tam was convinced that it would provide answers to some of the questions haunting her: Who was she? What was she doing with her life? What did she have to offer the world? Brittney insisted the workshop would provide insights into their true, beautiful, inner selves – well, that makes total sense when your animal spirit is a fricking butterfly.

Tam wasted twenty-five dollars. As a single mother of two, she didn't have that kind of money to spare. They would have to go without something this month because of her foolishness. She'd have to get the generic granola bars the kids complained so bitterly about and go without Red Box movies for a couple of weeks…no, that wasn't fair, this was her fault, not the kids'. She'd walk to work for the next couple of weeks, eat boiled eggs for lunch everyday, and give up coffee drinks for a while. This was all on her.

The more she dwelled on it, the more pissed she got, and to make matters worse, ever since she saw the stupid chicken in her vision, it had been following her – literally following her. She turned around and there it stood a few feet behind her, clucking.

How was this her spirit animal?

Tam started walking forward again and so did the chicken. She hoped it truly was a spirit animal and that no one besides her could see it.

When Tam stopped, the chicken stopped. She turned to see it pecking at pebbles embedded in the cement sidewalk. The pebbles weren't even food and they were never, ever going to come out. Tam waved her hands at the chicken. "Shoo. Go away. Shoo."

The chicken stood her ground, and the look in the chicken's eyes made Tam feel guilty. Coco didn't say anything specific about it, but Tam guessed you probably weren't supposed to shoo your spirit animal.

"Sorry, chicken. It looks like we're stuck with each other for a while, so we might as well get to the house and see if we can figure this out."

Back home, Tam sat alone at the dining room table and racked her brains to think of any chicken stories or symbolism she could remember. The chicken walked around the table, stopping occasionally to turn its head to the side in the weird sideways stare chickens sometimes do.

Tam's and her sister grew up hearing stories about the zodiac animals. Everyone in her family knew the basic details of their sign. Tam was a cat. Roosters were another one of the signs, but she was pretty sure it was specifically roosters, not chickens in general, and besides roosters and cats were not considered compatible.

Tam turned and leaned toward the chicken. "Are spirit animals connected to zodiac signs?"

The chicken's head bobbed up and waved side to side, just once, but it was enough for Tam to be sure it wasn't a zodiac thing.

Tam thought of The Little Red Hen, a story she had read to both of her kids when they were little. Technically, her chicken wasn't red, it was pasty white, but she was desperate and couldn't be splitting hairs. As she recalled the Little Red Hen made bread, by herself, from scratch.

Tam looked at the chicken who had strutted back over toward her. "I'm a hard worker and so is the Little Red Hen. Is that it? Is that why you're my spirit animal? Because we're both hard workers?"

By way of response, the chicken turned away from Tam and walked the other way, suddenly quite interested in some stray strands of dust.

"Okay, so that's not it."

She knew it wasn't, because the moral of The Little Red Hen was that all the animals in the hen's life were basically lazy, so the hen had to do everything herself. Although Tam worked hard, experience taught her that raising kids really did take a village, and she had plenty of support. Her parents, sister, neighbors, and friends all helped out. Even the kid's soccer coach was a godsend to their family.

Being chicken sometimes meant being afraid, but Tam knew she could cross that one right off. Single mothers didn't have the luxury of being scared. When you're the only parent around, you spend a lot of time looking under beds for boogey men. Tam didn't even bother to ask the chicken about that possibility.

Tam took out her phone and looked up chickens on Wikipedia. It turns out chickens are the most wide spread domesticated animal.

Tam looked at the chicken.

"Common? Domesticated? Is that what we're about?"

The chicken clucked and shook its head.

"Good. I was hoping that wasn't it."

Tam got up and walked to the living room. She sat in the faded green recliner her parents had passed down to her. The chicken, of course, followed and seemed happy to have a new place to explore and picked at individual strands in the shaggy area rug.

Tam thought about the legendary chicken who crossed the road to get to the other side.

"Practical? Or anti-humor?" Tam made air quotes with her fingers as she said 'anti-humor.'

The chicken didn't dignify that with a response. Chickens hate that joke.

Tam heard the back door bang shut, and, a few minutes later her tween-aged daughter Le breezed into the living room.

"Hi mom. How was your thing?"

"Hi Sweetheart. Turns out it was a mistake. I shouldn't have gone."

Le draped herself on the arm of the big recliner. "How so?"

"You'll never believe what my spirit animal is."

"What?"

"A chicken."

Le shrugged. "Makes sense to me."

"It makes sense to you that I'm a chicken?"

"Sure. Is it a white one? Like the kind that lay eggs and that you eat?"

"Yes."

Le nodded. "Makes perfect sense."

"Okay, dear daughter of mine, please explain to me how I'm a chicken."

"Mom, chickens do for others. They lay eggs, like forever, so people can have a cheap healthy food source. They sit on nests. They use their own body heat to hatch their babies. They barf up their own food so those babies can eat and they guard their chicks close. Then after all that, they're killed, cooked, and eaten. Chickens are all about sacrifice. They're the ultimate moms. Just like you."

Le gave her mom a quick kiss on the head and then propelled herself off the arm of the chair and toward the stairs that she bounded up two at a time.

Tam smiled and clutched her hands to her heart. Tears streaked her cheeks. She looked down at the chicken who had moved closer. The chicken looked Tam square in the eye and then jumped up, circled twice, and then settled down and roosted on Tam's lap and Tam was fine, absolutely fine, with that.

Flap

Keep, Goodwill, trash.

Bruce plotted League of Legends moves on this Friday night like all Friday nights, but instead of doing it in his comfy lounger with cold Coors and double cheese, double crust, fully loaded pizza, tonight, his game strategy ran through his head as he sorted dad's stuff. Dad died so unexpectedly it took time to get over the shock and get around to the many unpleasant details. As the only child and with mom out of the picture ages ago, all the drudgery fell to Bruce.

Who knew the man wore garter socks, bought management books from infomercial hacks, and bothered to transfer Richard Simons "Sweatin' to the Oldies" videos to DVD? The responsibility of wrapping things up annoyed and exhausted Bruce. He gazed around the room, almost done. What a relief.

One last thing. Bruce exhaled, squished down onto his belly, and checked under the bed. Something iridescent by the bedpost caught his eye. Bruce twisted, reached and pulled out—what? A super fancy gravy boat with a fitted lid? Weird.

Bruce considered the fate of the item. Keep, Goodwill or trash? He turned it over in his palm and ran his fingers across the glossy surface. Mid stroke a hissing sound and billowy blue smoke filled the room.

As the smoke dissipated it revealed a large blue man who definitely wasn't a man. He wore a turban complete with jewel and feather, a mask, a dark trimmed beard and mustache, a silky vest, flowing cape, what Bruce could only think of as "hammer pants," and pointy slipper shoes. His big smiling eyes somehow made him seem nonthreatening.

Bruce stared. After a few seconds the nonman spoke.

"I'm a Jinn, as in Genie."

Bruce involuntarily nodded. The guy sure fit the bill.

"Are you Scott's boy? You look like you could be."

Bruce nodded again.

"Okay, so, sorry for your loss. Your dad and I were in the middle of some business, and now it's your business. So good news! You get a wish. What's your name?"

"Bruce." This time Bruce didn't nod. "A wish?"

"Yep. Your dad had three and used two, so you inherit the last one."

"My dad used two wishes? What? Wait, is that how he died? Did wishing kill my dad?"

The question hung heavy for a few seconds before the Jinn broke eye contact and rubbed the back of his neck.

"So look kid, everything has gotten so litigious these days and believe it or not, even my line of business is no exception. I can't really share any details with you, you know, legally, but I can say, wish carefully. I wish more people did. I really do."

"What?"

"Oh, and here's the other thing. I specialize. See the cape and mask? I do superpower wishes. That's my thing. Pick a superpower and I'll grant it."

As a hard-core gamer, Bruce immediately thought of his League of Legends Champion Ready Rocket. The possibility of having amazing abilities like Rocket was the ultimate jackpot. No consideration necessary. Bruce knew his pick thanks to hours of contemplation, long late night debates, and countless daydreams.

"I'd like to fly."

The Jinn smiled. "Good choice. Done."

"Done?"

"Yep. You can fly."

"Really?"

"Really."

Bruce took two long steps to the window and bent down to open it.

"What are you doing? You are about to fly for the first time and you want to start on the second floor?"

Bruce turned, trying to process the question.

"Again, no legal advise, but maybe start small."

Bruce turned to face the hallway. He balled his right hand into a fist and thrust it in the air. He leaned forward aiming his body toward the doorway.

"Humans." The Jinn obviously meant it as an insult. "That's not how you fly."

"It's how Superman and Supergirl fly. Or do I maybe turn my hands down like Iron Man?"

Big sigh. "Superman, Supergirl, and Iron Man all have super-human strength. You don't. You got one wish and you chose the ability to fly. You don't just get super strength thrown in as part of the deal."

Now Bruce really strained to process.

"Look, I've been stuck in your dad's place for a while now and I want to get out of here and get on with things, so can I just tell you how the whole flying thing works?"

Bruce, still trying to sort out the super strength thing, thought this might be a trick...

didn't Jinn's have a reputation for being tricky? But all he could think to say was, "Okay."

"You flap."

"I flap?"

"Yeah, you know, your arms. Kind of like a bird. Hands work too, bending at the wrists."

"I flap like a bird?" The question came out angry.

Another big sigh. "Just try. Like this."

The Jinn extended his arms and pumped them up and down a few times.

Feeling ridiculous, Bruce flapped and rose a few inches off the floor. In shock he stopped and plopped down. He didn't exactly crash, but his knees bent on impact and his whole body wobbled, especially his stomach and chins. He flapped again harder and faster. This time he rose about three feet. "How do I go forward?"

"Lean the direction you want to go, forward, back, or sideways. It's a lot like controlling a Segway. About the same learning curve too. Flapping is the power. Leaning is the steering."

The motion was pretty much the same as jumping jacks. After about 30 seconds, it hurt. Bruce stopped, dropped and wobbled.

"It's hard," he said, breathing heavily.

"Yeah, it's an aerobic activity, about the same as running."

"Running? It's like running? This is stupid. What's the point? I mean, how far can I go?"

"Well, I'm no doctor, so don't take this as medical advice or anything, legalities you know, but you're not exactly what I'd call fit. I'd guess you could do a half a mile or so. Maybe two or three with conditioning."

"So you're saying I could go a half mile to say 7-11 or Gamestop, flapping the whole way, and I'd be tired when I get there? I suppose I'd be all sweaty too?"

"For sure."

"This is bullshit. What's the point?"

"You'd reduce your carbon footprint. Probably by a lot."

"Are you kidding me?"

"Kind of. But here's is the thing with you humans, you always want everything to be easy. I mean really, something as awesome as flying takes a little effort and suddenly it's shit and there's no point?"

A lecture? Really? He should have thrown the weird gravy boat lamp into the trash pile. Bruce wished more than ever for a regular League of Legends, recliner, pizza, beer, Ready Rocket Friday. It would have been better if this whole flying thing had never happened.

But the Jinn prattled on, gaining steam until his lecture exploded into a full-blown rant impossible to ignore.

"I've been around for a very long time and I'll let you in on a little secret. Did you know there was a time when people couldn't swim? Oh, people longed to explore the oceans, to connect with their aquatic brethren, to feel the waves around them, and something far more powerful than me gave them this. Gave humans the ability to swim, but oh, it was hard, it took effort. So the vast majority of you quickly abandoned it, and those of you who still swim do so in profane man made ponds filled with chemicals. Humans!"

After a short pause, in a slightly calmer voice, the Jinn said, "I can see that you're frustrated by all this Bruce, but believe me the wish game is no bowl of cherries either."

Bruce looked incredulous and said nothing.

"Sorry Bruce. I took it too far. I've been stuck in the lamp for a while and it get's to me."

Feeling the whole thing sucked, Bruce sulked and offered no such good sport, conciliatory words to the Jinn.

"Okay, you can fly, so fly or don't it's up to you. Work at it or don't, all up to you. You didn't get three wishes, most people do, but your situation is different. I'm guessing if you had, you'd of added super strength, but believe it or not you probably dodged a bullet there. It's a dangerous combination, but you humans always wish for dangerous stuff. Don't get me started on invisibility – so dangerous, or mind reading. Mind reading is the worst. You really don't want to know what people are thinking. You don't. But I can see you're feeling cheated. I can't give you another wish. It goes against all the rules, but here's a consolation prize. I can share some age-old wisdom with you, a real profound truth if you will. Interested?"

Bruce shrugged. He never imagined that an actual real-life magical creature could be so boring. He tried hand flapping, bending at the wrist. He found it even harder than arm flapping and only good for a few inches of lift.

"OK, here it is kid: humans almost always wish for things they can already do with just a little effort."

Hissing, blue smoke, and the Jinn was gone.

Bruce dropped and wobbled; as a modern guy, struggling to fly, he just couldn't bear such a heavy thought.

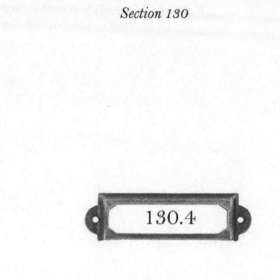

The Smile She Deserved

Oh, the ennui of being queen of the sea. A lone moody mermaid perched on her rookery and watched the island's only inhabitant, young Jacob. How she despised him. The only eligible male to come to her realm since she had come of age was in every way completely unworthy of her.

She warranted a strapping, athletic man with strong broad shoulders, golden hair, and sky-blue eyes. Her mate needed a smile that could and would affirm her beauty each and every time he looked upon her. This one amounted to an anchovy at best; short, little more than a boy, hair the color of mud, and spectacles that obscured his eyes so much that she could hardly care what color they were. To make matters worse, he spent inordinate amounts of time watching terns. He seemed to worship the birds – a sure sign he was simple in the head.

A small gust shook the mermaid from her reverie and she realized she wasn't alone in her study of the sea slug. A seal bobbing in the water not four feet away watched Jacob too with big innocent eyes. Although she looked like any ordinary seal, the Lorelei recognized the selkie, a maiden of the sea, inferior, but not so different from herself.

"Little sister, why do you waste your gaze on this ridiculous male?"

Without turning, the selkie answered, "I have decided to swim to him and offer him my skin and become his wife."

"Why would you give yourself to him? He is beneath even you."

"Perhaps, but it has been a long while and the only other male to come to this place is the withered one, with the barnacle beard. Yes, this one is puny, and weak, and unkempt, and inexplicitly attracted to sea birds, but I fear he is the best I can hope for."

The mermaid considered. She, of course, knew of old barnacle beard. He seemed to be a caretaker of sorts and never stayed long. Was the selkie right? Well, Jacob was the only option so, yes, that did make him the best option. The mermaid sighed expressing all the self-pity she suddenly felt. "You're right little one. I didn't see it until you pointed it out, but I must offer myself to him and become his wife."

"Wait a minute. You just said he wasn't even good enough for me. What are you saying now?"

"He is beneath us both, it's true, but I now see that it is a sin for me to not allow him to be with me. My beauty will not be denied. I must have him. I mean look at me. Am I not the very definition of resplendent? I dare not risk the terrible waste."

Sadly, the selkie couldn't argue with her logic. The mermaid was resplendent and it would indeed be a waste.

With a heart full of reservation and revulsion, the mermaid dove into the water and headed to shore. The selkie worried she had little chance against the mermaid, but she raced toward the shore as well, convinced that this was her one and only shot.

Deep in his tern data, Jacob did not expect to see two naked women in the cabin when he looked up.

The shorter, and to his mind, prettier one, held a wrinkly animal skin. She had thick brown hair, enormous brown eyes and a lean, toned build. Next to her stood a total Galamazon. If she hadn't been completely exposed Jacob might have mistaken her for a drag queen with her outrageously long locks and lashes. Where the littler one struck him well proportioned and unpretentious, this one seemed all curves and dazzle.

The selkie stepped forward holding her skin out toward Jacob. "You are small, odd, flawed in countless ways, and you reek of terns, but you are my only option for a mate. This is my skin. Build a fire and burn it and I will become your maid, your lover, and your wife."

Jacob shot up from his chair and stumbled backward.

The mermaid, not about to lose the upper hand, seized control of the situation. "Unfit as you are, I rank highest here, if anyone is having you as a mate, it is I."

She inhaled and then bellowed out a strange, haunting song. As her eerie, enchanted melody filled the room, everything turned hot, and slow, and woozy. The scent of rosemary wafted through the air, smoky and intoxicating. The mermaid composed herself regally, focused directly on Jacob and with all the sultriness that was her birthright and with the seductive authority vested in her by the power of the sea, sashayed toward him.

Jacob held his hand out in front of him.

"What are you doing?" he demanded.

The spell broke and the room turned back to normal.

Utter disbelief filled both the mermaid and selkie. This was all wrong. The mermaid was indignant. The selkie seemed confused and maybe a little turned on.

"How is this possible?" the mermaid snapped. "You are a man. We are siren. You can neither resist nor deny us."

"I'm pretty sure I just did."

"How is this possible?" The horrified mermaid repeated.

"Well, I can think of a couple reasons. For starters, I'm in a committed relationship, engaged in fact." The thought of his fiancé made Jacob grin. "And besides that, I'm gay."

"What do you mean gay?" The selkie broke in. "Do you mean happy? Like you're so gay with your engagement you can resist the allure of siren? Are you engaged to a witch?"

"No, to a man. I'm gay."

Jacob grabbed a framed picture off the shelf and extended it toward the bewildered women.

There in the photo embracing Jacob was the mermaid's Adonis – the muscles, the blond hair, the blue eyes, even the smile, but it was Jacob this man's smile affirmed.

Jacob couldn't help himself. "His name is Sven," he gushed, "Isn't he gorgeous? He's a competitive Nordic skier. He's training for the Olympics. I miss him so. He's such a hottie."

"You desire one the same as you? This happens?" The thought seemed to be blowing the poor selkie's mind.

The mermaid cut her off. "I'm the hottie here. And both of us are siren. You should not be able to resist either of us."

"Okay, let me get this straight. You," Jacob pointed to the selkie, "are only interested in me because no matter how lousy I am, you're pretty sure I'm the best you can do?"

The selkie nodded demurely.

"And you are only interested because she is and if anybody's going to get a man around here, it's going to be you, right?"

"That's hardly the point."

"To me it is. Thank God I'm gay, because I couldn't stand to be stuck with either of you."

"Are you sure you're gay?" The mermaid countered.

"Yes. I'm sure."

"How are you sure?"

"If you must know, I tried having a girl-friend. She was a great girl. We're still friends and all. It just didn't work out."

"You laid with a woman, even though you de-sired a male in your heart? Was she a hottie too?" The selkie asked.

"Yeah, some people can handle being bisex-ual, it was worth a shot, but not for me. She was pretty enough, and smart, and kind, but turns out it's only guys for me."

The mermaid refused to accept any of this and with no subtly whatsoever assaulted Jacob with every trick she had. She attacked with sul-try come-hither eyes, slow seductive motions, and shamelessly obscene postures.

Jacob hardly noticed any of it, but she at-tracted the selkie's full attention.

"Sorry girls. Go back to the sea. I am not the one for either of you."

"No. No, you're not." The selkie agreed. And with that the selkie led the confounded mermaid back to the watery depths where they belonged.

"You really are beautiful." The selkie offered.

"Yes, I know," the mermaid agreed.

"I mean you're a hottie for sure."

"Yes, yes I am."

"I have no idea why anyone would try to contest your charms."

"Neither do I."

"Maybe I can catch us some crabs and we can talk more?"

She thought that would be nice. She said, "Yes, you may enjoy my company."

The selkie reached the water's edge.

"I think we can both still do better than barnacle beard."

The mermaid laughed spreading radiance across her being. She was a vision. The selkie smiled back. The mermaid took notice, and looked closely, studying the smile. Something inside the Lorelei stirred as she realized this was the kind of smile she'd been waiting for, the one she knew she deserved.

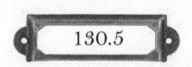

Hardly Any Feel Left

Tired and hungry, Zach finally found a perfect place to make camp, perfect except for the zombie.

The sad rotting corpse struggled against a tangled fence, attempting the same step over and over. He moaned and flailed toward Zach, but he was good and stuck and wasn't going anywhere.

Zach knew he should bash the poor bastard's head in, but he was so tired of bashing heads. Zach felt beaten. Exhausted by the hopelessness, the meaninglessness, worn-out from being afraid, from being angry, and most of all from being alone. These days everyone was dead or an asshole, and neither made good company. Assholes in particular tended to lie, steal, and threaten, so at the moment the trapped dead guy wasn't looking so bad.

The zombie seemed young to Zach, probably around his own age and he didn't appear too decayed, so Zach figured he hadn't been dead long. Zach made polite conversation as unloaded his backpack and set up for the night.

"I'm Zach, twenty-years-old, from the Muskegon area. I had a job at Best Buy. I'm pretty sure everyone I know is dead. You?"

The zombie groaned.

"Yeah. It sucks. Everything sucks. You look quite stuck. You been like that a while? I'd set you loose, but you'd for sure try to eat me and I'm beyond sick of people trying to eat me…it's so weird, everyone trying to eat everyone all the time."

As Zach spoke, he looked around. They were in an abandoned tree farm. Zach had picked his way through a mishmash of miniature trees—rows of baby maples, oaks, and elms standing across from an array of their conifer cousins—to reach the large uncultivated field where he now prepared to spend the night. The journey through the strange landscape that was both perfectly organized and starting to become overrun felt surreal, like everything these days.

The field separated the nursery from a barn, house, and an assortment of other outbuildings. Zach strung safety wire around a boulder, an old fence post, and a couple of saplings, and then laced it with items intended to clang if bumped to wake him. He rolled out a tattered green sleeping bag in the middle of his little territory and sat on it. He pulled a granola bar, cellphone, and gadget from his pack and connected the phone to the little machine.

"You can't imagine how happy I am that I bought this solar charger right before it all starting going down." Zach said between bites. "Such dumb luck. Sweet employee discount too. Lots of my apps still work. Thank God for automation. I used to be against it, what with what it did to all the good assembly line jobs and all, but these days I've changed my tune. That's for sure." Zach crumbled the granola bar wrapper and unplugged his phone from the charger.

"Let's selfie."

Zach stood a safe distance in front the ensnared zombie who grabbed and growled, but truthfully the rank smell of spoiling flesh alone was good enough reason for a few feet between them. Zach held up the phone framing himself and the zombie, shook most of the dirt off his mop of brown hair, opened his brown eyes wide, and smiled exposing perfectly aligned teeth. Even under a thick layer of grime he looked good. It was hard to say for sure, but it seemed like Zach and Zombie might have passed for kin at some point not too long ago. They had the same build. Zach snapped the picture and laughed at the thought of a shirttail zombie relative. "Are you my brother from another mother?"

The zombie snorted.

"Dude, I may have something for you." Zach ruffled through his pack and produced a Christmas tree air freshener, like people hang in their cars. He took careful aim and tossed it at the zombie. It landed just as Zach had hoped, snagged on what was left of the zombie's tattered polo shirt collar.

"Maybe that'll help."

As he settled back into his little camp, Zach fussed with his phone and charger and said, "I wonder if you were a geeky guy too. You look like you might have been."

The zombie grunted.

"Did you just respond to me? Were you a geek? You were, weren't you?"

Another grunt.

"I may have lost my God damned mind, but I think you're talking to me."

"Urrrrrrrr……" said the zombie with a creepy nod.

"Okay, here goes nothing. Google translate," Zach said to his phone, "can you speak zombie?"

"Yes." The sultry, but cold digital female phone voice answered.

"Ha! Should've known." Zach thrust the phone in the zombie's direction. "Zombie, what's your name?"

The zombie let out a long hissing exhale that sounded like "sssssaaander," to Zach.

"Xander," the phone announced.

"Oh my God, is your name Xander?"

The next murmured exhale the phone translated as, "yes."

"And you can really understand me? You are talking to me?"

"Yes."

"If you can talk and think, why are you stuck on that fence? Why can't you get yourself free?"

After a much longer series of groans, the phone translated, "Slow. Took me long time to know stuck, probably take long time to know how to unstuck. Plus all motor skills gone to hell."

Zack giggled with glee. This was the best conversation he'd had in weeks.

"Well, Xander, tell me all about yourself. Where are you from? Did you have a job? A family? What's your story?"

After another series of utterances, the phone said, "Hard. Hard to remember before."

"You've lost your memories? That sucks."

"No, not hard here," the zombie bonked himself on the head, "hard here." He thumped near his heart.

"You mean it's hard for you to talk about, like painful?"

The zombie let out another whispery breath that the phone translated as, "Yes."

"Wow. I've been hating you guys for weeks. I never imagined you could be suffering. I thought about smacking your head off when I first saw you.

Sorry."

"No worries. Not suffering now. Only hurts when try remember."

"You're not in pain now? Like this very moment?"

"No."

"Oh. Do you want to eat me?"

"Yes."

"What the hell Xander? Don't you feel bad about that? Doesn't it upset you that you want to eat people?"

"No."

"Why the hell not? Maybe I should smash you."

It took a minute to translate the longer moan talk, but eventually the female phone voice said, "Maybe. Eating feel good. Best part of life after. Hardly any feel left. Why feel bad about feel good?"

"Eating people makes you feel good?"

"Yes."

"How do you not feel terrible about that?"

Zach could have sworn, Xander half shrugged.

"Eat cow, pig, chicken before. Feel good, probably wouldn't if thought too much, but didn't. Family eat animals, teach me eat animals, always eat animals. Feel good. You eat animals?"

"Of course I do. I'm from Michigan. I hunt deer and love me some hotdogs and brats."

"Feel good?"

"Yes."

"So?"

"Eating animals is not the same as eating people."

"Oh. Sorry. Same for me."

Things went quiet. Zach felt tense, so he just thought for a while.

"Xander?"

"Yes?"

"Do you want me to kill you? Like, bop you in the brain? Put you out of your misery?"

"No."

"No? You want to stay a zombie?"

"Not so bad being zombie."

"Not so bad? You're stuck on a fence. You want to eat me. That's not so bad?"

"Zach, you want die? You want me kill you? Put out of misery?"

"No! Of course not."

"Is not so bad? Not so bad stuck inside wire circle? Not so bad scared zombie eat? Not so bad, alone?"

Zach understood Xander's point and he did not like it. "How is it not so bad being a zombie?"

"Before, crap job. Before, jerk boss. Before, parent basement. Before, bust car. Before, 9 to 5. Before, grind. Now, no worry, no work, no problems, just eat and feel good. Being zombie not so bad. When you zombie, not so bad."

"Wait, doesn't it hurt for you to remember stuff?"

"Not that stuff. Pain when remember girlfriend. Pain when remember birthday. Pain when remember baseball homerun."

"Yeah, I was a ball player too. I know what you mean. So are you telling me to not lose sleep over becoming a zombie? That it's not that bad?"

"Yes. Except…"

"What?"

"Except, almost no feel. Feel good when eat, but no feel bad, no feel curious, no feel happy, no feel surprise, no feel friendship. Mostly just no feel. Bummer."

"Hmm." Zach laid thinking. As he dozed off his head whirled with perspectives he had never considered.

Zach woke early and packed up camp.

"Xander, I'm taking off. I'm not going to kill you, mostly because you don't want me to. I'd love to let you loose and keep you around for company, the air freshener seems to be helping a little bit, but you'd try to eat me wouldn't you?"

"Yes."

"I thought so. Too bad, you seem like an okay guy. Best I've met in a while anyways."

"Thank."

Zach started to walk away deep in thought and then stopped and turned back toward the zombie.

"Xander, do you think I should end it? Go ahead and let you eat me? Become a zombie?"

Xander took longer than usual to answer.

"I would like eat Zach, but no. No become zombie now."

"Why not?"

"Zach still have time."

"Time for what?"

"Time for feel. Go feel sad, feel curious, feel happy, feel surprise, feel friendship. Feel all while you can."

Believe

Kerri invited Chris on a cryptozoology-cele-brate-Champy-the-lake-monster weekend to test their fledgling relationship.

The drive from Cambridge to Burlington flew by. Every hour Chris became more interesting. Every mile uncovered something new they had in common. They both loved the Replacements, lived through being a middle child, and found all forms of squash inedible. In Chris's company, the simple futon in her sister and brother-in-law's living room felt romantic. He went along with every one of her crazy plans for the trip smiling the whole way.

They laughed and held hands through all of yesterday's big event, a street fair and sidewalk sale on the New York side of Lake Champlain. A lunch of charred Champy burgers, greasy lakeside fries, and a green mint lake monster milkshake – one shake, two straws, tasted exquisite when shared with Chris at an old fashion beachside picnic table-type joint. They watched amused but respectful as a resident musician performed an original Champy song, a musical rendition of the "Plesiosaurus theory" held by most locals.

Kerri cleaned out the Champy crafts and swag table manned by the musician's girlfriend. Her take included an EP of the Champy song, a self-published book, Champy, the Lake Moster Revealed, complete with a misspelling on the cover, a ceramic Champy toothbrush holder—Kerri's favorite find, and matching Champy t-shirts for her and Chris. That night they ate and drank their way through the charming Church Street neighborhood with Kerri's sister and brother-in-law and ended the evening with late-night video games and drinks back at the condo. Chris had been fun, engaged, and attentive through all or it. She could not have wished for more.

This morning, after devouring a tower of gooey nacho spuds for brunch they rented a boat and rowed around the lake ready for an up close Champy encounter. Kerri brought along her recently purchased copy of Champy, the Lake Moster Revealed, and read a few of the kookier eyewitness accounts out loud. Chris looked hot in his new Champy shirt.

For the first time all weekend the conversation lagged. They stopped rowing, took a break from telling the all important "getting to know you" stories that were bringing them closer and closer together, and just drifted on the lake. Kerri let her fingertips drag just below the water's surface, cool and pleasant. She ogled Chris, hoping her sunglasses would make it less obvious. What a good-looking guy. His mixed Chinese and African heritage resulted in creamy caramel skin, deep brown eyes, and a lean strapping stature. She marveled at her good fortune that he was there with her.

He beamed right at her. Busted. He caught her starring. She laughed embarrassed. To break the tension, she tapped the surface the lake and called, "Champy, here, Champy, Champy, Champy." They both laughed.

"I love you," Chris blurted, caught up in the moment with this awesome, funny, gorgeous girl.

He loves me. He said it. Stunned in the best sort of way, Kerri smiled. Her heart pounded and mind raced. The cliché of it all shocked her even more. What a beautiful, perfect moment. She wanted to say it back. She definitely felt it, but an enormous green-grey head atop a human-sized section of muscular neck gracefully rose from the water two feet off the left side of the boat. It was Champy no doubt. She looked just like the drawing on Chris's shirt.

She watched Kerri and Chris as Kerri and Chris eyed her. No one moved.

After thirty eternal seconds Kerri broke the spell by pulling her phone out of her pocket. She tapped the camera app and tried to snap a picture, but her hand shook.

In sharp contrast to the way she had emerged, Champy's head snapped back under the surface with the sharp whip of a retracting tape measure. The hasty retreat caused a wake that pitched the boat into an uncontrollable wobble.

"Crap. My phone."

Chris's hand shot out and grabbed it before it hit the drink.

"Oh. My. God." Champy occupied every bit of her consciousness. She had just seen a lake monster.

She snatched the phone from Chris's hand and scrolled. She had gotten a pic...of something.

It didn't look like much and certainly didn't look like a lake monster. The fuzzy image mostly looked like a greenish-grey rock hitting the surface. With nothing but water and the rock-head in the photo there wasn't even a perspective for the size of the thing.

But it didn't matter. Kerri knew what it was. She saw a lake monster, a real, live lake monster. They both did and they had proof – sort of. Her mind caught on "they"– Chris! Oops, in her excitement, she'd totally forgotten about Chris.

"Chris. I don't believe it. It's amazing…We just saw Champy. She's real."

"Soooo cool, but of course she is. Didn't you already know that? Isn't that why we came?"

"I mean, yeah…we came to see her…you know, sort of like she was real, but she is real. I mean, really real. We really, really saw her."

"Are you saying that you didn't believe in her before?"

"I think I did. I mean, I guess I wanted to believe in her, but now I do. I mean, how could I not? We saw her. Everything's changed."

"What's changed?"

"Everything." Kerri yelled without meaning to. "We have to tell people. We have to show them."

"We do?"

"Of course."

"Who do we need to tell and what do we need to tell them?"

"Everyone. Everyone needs to know that's she's real."

"Lots people already know. We spent all day yesterday at a festival full of people who knew. You just read pages from your book about people who also saw her."

"But this is different. It's us. We know. Don't you think that's different?"

"I already knew. Not one hundred percent, but I was pretty sure. I guess that's why I'm not freaking out."

"You're not, are you? Wow, here I thought I was the true believer, but I guess you were all along. But Chris, come on, get excited. We need to share this with the world. It's so important."

"It's important yes, but I am not going share it with the world. I'm not planning to tell anyone."

"Are you crazy? Why not?"

"Because I care."

"You think I don't? I do. I mean, what about scientists? They need to know. They need to study her and, you know, improve her habitat. That sort of thing."

"Her habitat seems fine now. How do you think they would study her? Isolate her? Capture her? Take samples? Or worse. I think she just made it pretty clear that she doesn't even want her picture taken. And imagine we were somehow able to convince a scientist that she's real and then word got out. Do you think Champy tours and chatzky stands would improve her habitat?"

She wanted to snap back. The thrill of seeing Champy was still coursing through her and she was far too excited for Chris's rational thoughts. Her body needed fight or flight or something. How could he think so clearly? He really was perfect and he was right on every count. She felt unworthy of his recent declaration of love. He had said "I love you," and she hadn't responded at all. Instead she had argued with him. He said "I love you" and she picked a fight, their first fight. What if it were their last? The thought "what an idiot I am," materialized in her head, but she felt it, deep and harsh in the gut.

"Chris, I'm so sorry. I'm blowing it aren't I? I'm ruining everything. You said 'I love you' and I didn't say it back, even though I do. I do, I love you, but it's lame to say it now."

"No it isn't. And anyway I kind of knew. Just like Champy, I wasn't one hundred percent, but I was pretty sure. Seeing her doesn't make it her any more or less real and hearing you say the words doesn't make them any more or less true. Wanting to believe in something isn't the same as believing in something and I for one believe in us."

This time it was Kerri who sent the boat rocking as she launched herself at him; enough talk.

After a wet and wild make-out session they sat holding one another, exhausted but happy, looking out over the glassy lake.

"Someday we'll bring our kids here," Chris said. "And our grandkids. We'll tell them this is where it all started. We came here, saw a lake monster, had a fight and fell in love. We figured it all out right here."

Just to let them know she approved, and that they'd gotten their priorities straight, Champy poked her head back up and gave them the lake monster version of a smile.

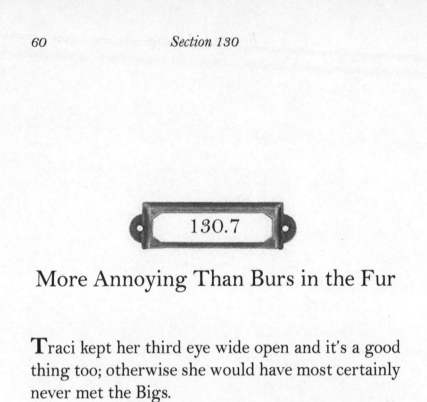

130.7

More Annoying Than Burs in the Fur

Traci kept her third eye wide open and it's a good thing too; otherwise she would have most certainly never met the Bigs.

Over the summer Traci found herself domestically challenged, so she spent forty-three intentional days, realigning her chakras, deeply exploring her Virgo nature, and generally rethinking her priorities in a tent in Point Park. Rangers on the lookout for squatters posing as campers pushed her into some of deeper, less hospitable areas of the park, where the Bigs resided – definitely the best thing that ever happened to her.

However, no matter how blissful the summer had been, and it had been, a little over a month of soul searching revealed she was ready to get back to civilization in general and into an apartment in particular. So she got her shit together and found two jobs, one for easy money, hotel maid, and the other to feel good about, telemarketer for Action-Now.

Today, the first day after the first full moon, her favorite day, she braided her long hair, donned her recycled sari skirt, which provided life-changing employment to artisan women in India, and made her routine COSTCO run for a barrel of cheese puffs and case of assorted jerkies. Then she headed back to her former home, Point Park.

It was a forty-minute drive with rough terrain near the end. If human, her car would have been old enough to legally buy booze or even pot here in Washington State, and a tune-up was long overdue, but as long as Mercury stayed out of retrograde Traci knew her sweet old Civic would hold together.

She parked at a campsite and hiked to the big tree where she knocked and hooted. The Bigs knocked and hooted back – the Discovery Channel had gotten this part right. After a few minutes Spicy Cheetos, the female, emerged from the forest. Traci always teared up at the stunning, primordial sight.

Traci put her COSTCO items on the ground and placed her hands in prayer position at her heart center. Traci bowed her head and said, "My mother, my sister, my daughter, my friend, I honor you and greet you, and rejoice that the Universe has brought us together once more."

Spicy replied, "hi," and in one swift and clever maneuver gathered Traci into her enormous embrace and took possession of the COSTCO goods. Then they walked cockeyed arm and arm into the woods.

Danger Don't Enter, the male, grunted a greeting as the women entered the clearing. Little Harry, the juvenile giggled and looked away shyly. Danger hugged Traci, letting his hands slide down until he was cupping her ass and gave it a good long squeeze. It always made Traci uncomfortable, but she would have rather died than insult another's culture and she was certain that this was their traditional greeting. It wasn't, unless one counted Danger's personal greeting for Traci.

Traci so loved the company of the Bigs and they so loved the snacks she always brought. Spicy munched salty cheese puffs by the handfuls and the boys gnawed on the tough jerky sticks.

"How are things?"

"Okay. Too many campers though; they are catching a lot of the perch and we want the fresh perch this time of year." Spicy complained.

"Too many squirrels too." Danger added.

"Yes, too many squirrels," Spicy agreed, "more annoying than burs in the fur. We found a huge stash of their acorns and spent a whole afternoon seeing if we could throw them hard and fast enough to kill the little beasts." All three Bigs guffawed. Traci squirmed, but knew she could not judge them by her limited human values.

"How many did we get, Danger? Four, five?"

"Five. Mostly old ones, but a couple of their wretched offspring too. Hoot, that was fun."

Traci was visibly uncomfortable, so Spicy changed the subject. "I found a new book, *On Walden Pond.* It's a little slow so far."

Traci admired how the Bigs taught themselves English, by reading park signs, labels on trash, and the occasional book they found. Spicy and Danger named themselves after favorite finds. Little Harry's name on the other hand was a joke. It sent the Bigs into fits of laughter the first time they described little, hairy, Little Harry to Traci. They laughed even harder when they added that he would someday be big and hairy and he would still be called "Little Harry." Their humor, so pure and joyful, touched Traci deeply.

The small talk was a gift as always, but Traci needed to discuss something important with them and she was not going to wimp-out this time.

"Poo-poo-poo-poo-poo," Little Harry chanted as he squatted over a log and took a dump. He laughed uproariously at the sloppy, wet, vibrating sound of excrement and air squirting out.

As the odor wafted toward Traci, pungent, but organic, she looked at Harry with adoration, the way one looks at a puppy. He is truly one with nature, so pure, so beautiful, she thought. On a more practical level she was grateful for the pause it caused in the conversation and took advantage of it.

"Spicy, Danger, I have something I want to talk to you about."

They both turned and looked at her.

"I want to bring you back with me to civilization." She continued on quickly, knowing if she paused, they'd object. "I know we've talked about it before and you weren't interested, but things have changed now. I've figured everything out. I had to juggle things financially to afford the membership, but I joined a group called PETA, People for the Ethical Treatment of Animals, and I know they will embrace you. It wouldn't just be me, a whole army of like-minded people are waiting to welcome you to the world. There is so much I want to share with you, so much for you to see and do and learn."

"We're not animals and we're welcome just fine in the world." Spicy said matter-of-factly.

Oh Goddess, I've insulted them. "Of course, but, but, the PETA people would still help you because they're...compassionate like me. They love all their fellow creatures."

The look in Spicy's eyes made it clear that she wasn't thrilled by the word "creatures" either, but she simply said, " No Traci, we are not interested in going with you."

"I know you're scared by the idea, but I would protect you."

"Bigs aren't scared."

"Well, no, of course not, you are so powerful and empowered, but what I mean is, humans have a violent history, it's only natural to fear human savagery."

"Traci, we eat baby bunnies for breakfast after we rip their heads off with our teeth. Last night we swung a live deer fawn around by the legs, bashing it into trees in order to tenderize it before we ate it. We have no problem with savagery."

"But still, I know you must be scared of humans. I would never let them hurt you."

"No human has ever hurt a Bigfoot. Piss off a Bigfoot and you won't live to tell about it. We're not scared of humans."

Genuinely confused Traci asked, "What is it then? Why won't you come with me?"

"Traci, I…we don't want to hurt your feelings dear, but the truth is, we have no desire to be around humans because you're stupid."

Stupid? Relief passed through Traci. They didn't understand. That's all. This would be easy to clear up.

"Oh, Spicy, let me explain. Humans are different than you. Different is scary and confusing, but not stupid."

"No Traci, let me explain to you. I know what different means and yes, humans are different, but they are also very stupid."

Traci could have sworn she heard Danger say something like, "and condescending," under his breath, but that wasn't possible.

"Okay, I'm sensing bad energy. Can we all just join hands, breathe, and reconnect for a minute?"

Danger snorted. Spicy held up her orange powder covered hands and shrugged. Little Harry gleefully yelled out, "Poo-boom-boom," emphasizing the "boom-boom" by lifting and dropping his bottom into the mess he had made. He giggled hysterically and dropped onto the dirt chanting "Poo-boom-boom..." He scooted across the ground toward Traci holding out his hand, thrusting his bum on every "boom-boom," his chant frequently interrupted by peels of his own laughter. Right before reaching her he pulled back his hand and changed direction.

His innocence touched Traci as it always did, but right now she needed to clear up this misunderstanding she was having with Spicy and Danger.

"What makes you think humans are stupid?"

"We don't think, we know, but let me give you an example. You live in boxes."

"You mean houses?"

"You have lots of names for them, house, apartment, condo, trailer, but they are what they are, boxes. Humans live inside the box, Bigs don't. Even when you come here to the wilds you bring them with you – big metal ones on wheels – even you lived in a small flimsy one while you were in the forest."

The Bigs were smart, so it perplexed Traci that they couldn't understand houses. Why didn't they understand something so fundamental? Why was this all going so wrong? Traci instinctively reached for her necklace pendent, a crystal she always wore that imbued clarity and vision, but it wasn't there. How could she not be wearing it? She wore it religiously. And then she realized. It was so simple. It was the necklace. How could she possibly be clear, how could she share a vision without her crystal? Jeez, it's almost like Spicy was right, how stupid could she be trying to convince them to make a radical move like that without her necklace? Traci had to laugh at herself and yes, at her own stupidity.

"Poo-boom-boom, Poo-boom-boom."

Spicy ticked on her fingers, as she listed more proof of human stupidity. "You confine animals for companionship and never eat them..."

"Cats are worse than squirrels," Danger chimed in.

"...You pollute your own homes, you scrape the hair off your bodies, you worship your small plastic cell phones..."

It was time to go. Trying to convince them without her crystal was pure silliness.

"...You eat poisonous mushrooms all the time..."

"It's true. Humans can't tell a morel from a poisonpie." Danger interjected shaking his head.

Wait, now that she thought about it wasn't today the fifth day of the fifth month? She hadn't considered numerology at all. She was feeling more and more foolish by the minute. She needed to get in touch with Stan, her numerologist, right away.

"...you use machines to cut grass for no other reason than to throw it away, you determine dominance by who has the most pieces of paper money, you di-vorce, you catch perch and only eat half, you wear underpants..." Spicy droned on, but Traci was too distracted to listen.

Thank the Goddess she had gone with her gut and bought the Personal Power Nubian Pyramid. The tune up for the car and the visit to the dermatologist could both wait...they were just funny freckles after all. She'd have to call in sick, but some serious Pyramid meditation would probably redirect this whole situation. An astrology reading made total sense too, for something this important. And a tarot reading never hurt. If she hurried she could make it to the payday loan store before they closed.

With renewed energy Traci hugged the Bigs good-bye and practically jogged toward her car with excitement. Little Harry stopped boom-scooting, looked up and said, "Boom-boom bye Auntie Traci. Boom-boom bye." Spicy and Danger stared at him slack jawed. It was his first real complete sentence.

Spicy looked at the barrel of cheese puffs and sighed. She hated to lose her snack connection, but clearly this influence had gone too far. She'd have to savor this batch and make last as long as she could.

Tooth Exchange International Consultants

"**R**eport to HR. They're waiting for you."

Crap. Two weeks until the end of the probation period. The last month seemed better. Why now?

"How were your rounds tonight?"

"Good." Crystal turned in twenty-three teeth, an empty money belt, and associated paperwork. She didn't need directions to HR.

"In here, Ms. Ni." Priscilla waved her in. Damn, the Head of HR, it must be major.

Priscilla was a tough-ass. She was also a pixie. Crystal found conversations with pixies challenging. They were small and pointy, smelled like sap, and spoke in the pitch of someone sucking helium. To make matters worse, a Brownie sat next to Priscilla. Two tinies in the same meeting – double crap.

"Ms. Ni, this is Bob. He's from the Social Media Division. Do you know why we're here?"

Crystal imagined several possibilities, but feigned ignorance for fear of making matters worse. She widened her eyes in her best expression of innocence, one she had mastered over hundreds of years, and asked, "What's up?"

Brownies waste no time, so in response Bob leapt onto the desk, which was midway between fairy and human sized, like a small child's station, and swiveled a monitor as tall as himself around so that Crystal could see the screen. In a Munchkin voice, high, but not as high as Priscilla's, Bob announced, "This showed up on Facebook today."

A note, written by a child's hand filled the screen. It had to be one of her assignments'. It read:

Don't let your parents know.
Hey Meg, I need a favor. I lost two teeth and I tried to get the Tooth Fairy to take them and leave me money but she's not taking them, so can you put my two teeth under your pillow and give me the money she gave you knowing it was mine? Please? The two teeth are in the bag. Please don't take the money for yourself. (I know you wouldn't, but in case.)

The letter concluded with a drawing of a wide-mouthed girl missing two teeth.

Crystal found the post charming, but knew Priscilla and the organization did not. She braced herself.

"Ms. Ni, Do you know our mission statement here at TEIC, Tooth Exchange International Consultants?" Priscilla peeped.

Crystal knew that Priscilla knew she knew it. All RTCs, Regional Tooth Coordinators, underwent a mandatory, intensive, two-week training. In one long exhale, Crystal recited, "Tooth Exchange International Consultants support the office of The Tooth Fairy and instill a sense of comfort, wonder, and fiscal literacy in children around the world, regardless of race, religion, or political affiliation, through the exchange of teeth for currency."

"That's right, Ms. Ni. We exist for two essential reasons: to ease the burden of our primary client, The Tooth Fairy and to make kid's lives better with a little joy and magic. When we fail to exchange, when that failure is made public, when other children and even parents get involved, do you think we are succeeding at our most fundamental responsibilities?"

"No."

"No, we are not." Priscilla pounded her petite fist on the desk in fairy furry, but the tiny tap was hard to take seriously. The reality that this represented Crystal's third strike in as many months loomed much larger for her.

Priscilla squeaked on. "This is a black eye on the organization and you need to fix it. Fast."

Crystal was sure that Priscilla outfitted herself in power suits, towering hairdos, and severe make-up because she was aware that her diminutive size undermined her authority, especially with human-sized and near-human-sized fairies like Crystal. Priscilla meant business.

"I will not let a near-size, with big cow eyes, jeopardize my reputation or standing within the organization. You "bigs" get all the good jobs. Everything is so much easier for you, but you are not going to screw things up for me. I've arranged coverage for your entire caseload. You have until the end of your probation period to solve this. And let me be perfectly clear, if you can't, you will be terminated with no option for rehire."

As Crystal got up to leave, Bob threw in his parting shot, "And make sure, no more media."

Well, at least they hadn't figured out the worse part, not yet anyway. Crystal needed this job. It wasn't the greatest gig; far from it, but thanks to climate change fairy opportunities were dwindling. Her youth rapport ratings were pretty high – she'd have to try and work it out with the kid.

The gush and gurgle of running water helped Crystal think, so she went to her favorite Indonesian restaurant with a fountain in the dinning room. Spicy food comforted Crystal. With each swallow she extinguished a tiny curry flame, as she studied the client's paperwork.

Adopted from Ethiopia, the child Sheba lived most of her life in Tacoma, Washington. The file described a bright girl, with lots of friends, and diverse interests, including recently, roller derby. Well, that might explain the scheduling glitches with the teeth. There was an older letter in the file. In barely legible writing, at age four the child had written a saga about losing her first baby tooth in a Subway sandwich and accidently swallowing it, but could she please have the money anyway? Crystal headed to Sheba's house encouraged; the kid might be a little obsessed with money, but was clearly a good communicator and seemed reasonable.

"Sheba, wake up." Crystal whispered with a gentle shake.

"Huh?"

"Do you know who I am?"

Sheba rubbed her eyes. "Who are you? How did you get into my room? Why isn't Apple barking?"

"Dogs recognize us. We have an understanding. I'm a tooth fairy. Well, sort of. I'm actually a RTC, a Regional Tooth Coordinator." Crystal nodded her head from side to side on every other word as if that might somehow make the title make more sense. "But the important part is I work for The Tooth Fairy. Well, you know, in a consulting capacity."

Roused from a deep sleep, the only thing Sheba got out of Crystal's babble was 'Tooth Fairy.'

"I've been waiting. You're two teeth behind. But they're not here. They are at my friend Meg's. I asked her to turn them in after you never showed up here to take them."

"Yeah, I know."

"Then why are you here? Shouldn't you be at Meg's house? Can you give me the money without the teeth? I didn't think that's how it worked."

"No, it doesn't. I don't have any money anyway. I already burned through my whole budget for this month. Even my discretionary funds."

Sheba had no idea what discretionary funds were, but this did not sound good. "Am I being punished? Did I do something wrong? I really need that money."

Even though it was none of her business, Crystal couldn't help but wonder what a nine-year-old "needed" money for. "Why's the money so important?"

"I've been saving for an Xbox forever. I'm only ten dollars away from having enough. Those teeth should get me two bucks closer."

"Well, that's a problem Sheba, because I simply don't have the money to pay for them, and if I can't work this out with you, I'm fired."

"I don't want to get you in trouble, but we kid's have limited ways to make money…my birthday and gotcha day have already happened this year and Christmas isn't for months. What am I supposed to do?"

"Look kid, couldn't you help me out? Not to be insensitive, but I think I need my job more than you need two dollars, or even an Xbox for that matter."

"Why? Aren't you magic? Can't you just fix things with your magic?"

"I wish. I've been around for centuries and I'll tell you, there used to be a lot more magic in this world than there is now." In desperation Crystal decided she'd have to trust this kid. "If I tell you a secret, do you promise to keep it and not tell anyone?"

Sheba worried that her chances of an Xbox were slipping away, but the idea of a fairy secret was pretty exciting.

"I promise. What is it?"

Crystal swallowed hard. She hadn't admitted this out loud to anyone, ever. "I'm not a fairy. I lied on my application to get this job. I'm a naiad, a water nymph, not so different from a fairy, but more like a fairy cousin than an actual fairy and any magic I have is water-specific. I had a great life for hundreds of years. I had a modest stream, the Black River. It was small, but it provided all the power and magic I needed and I took care of it and its creatures in exchange. In 1916 humans built a ship canal and dried my little creek right up." Naiad tears originate deep beneath the Earth. They are deceptively small for the emotional torrent they carry and Crystal's were flowing. "I've been scraping to get by ever since. I can't go back to nature. It's too depressing. There's nothing left. The joy of children is the best substitute I've ever found for what really makes a naiad happy."

Affected, Sheba racked her brains to think of a way to help the naiad. "What about Easter?"

"What about it?" Crystal tried to stop sobbing.

"Well, it's only a few weeks away. I usually get clothes, sports stuff, and candy for Easter, but maybe the Easter Bunny could be convinced to bring me cash instead this year. Do you know him?"

She didn't, but the kid might be on to something. Maybe the Easter Bunny could help. "If I got the Easter Bunny to bring you at least ten bucks this year, would we be square for the teeth?"

"Yes."

"Okay. It's a plan. I'm off to find that big bunny. Thanks for working with me on this, Sheba. You're a good kid."

"Your welcome, and you're a beautiful Naiad. I'm sorry about your river. You shouldn't lie about who you really are. My dad says it's important to always tell the truth. I hope you can find a way to do that."

RTC's did not attend or even get invited to the annual conference for "Children's Holiday and Magical Creatures," but everyone knew about it. Crystal located a copy of last year's symposium booklet and, Bingo, she had the contact info she needed. One quick call and she found herself waiting for a face-to-face at Easter Command Central located on a large river island. The place put her at ease.

"EB will see you now, Ms. Ni."

She had picked out a sheer dress with pastel stripes hoping to make a good impression. "Thank you for agreeing to see me."

"Come in. Come in Ms. Ni."

"Crystal, Please."

"Charmed Crystal. Please call me EB. Have a seat. What brings you to ECC today?

Crystal seated herself in a wicker chair across from EB. "A current client case, actually. I'm hoping you can help me."

"Unusual, but not unheard of for caseloads to overlap, but, no offense, on the few rare occasions when they have, I typically meet with someone a bit more...senior...in the organization, I mean."

"Um, no offense taken. No one from TEIC knows I'm here. Not my boss Priscilla, and certainly not the big boss. I'm trying to work out a tricky case. I have a lot riding on it."

"Oh, Priscilla's your boss? I know her well, and the big boss too. We had some fun times at last year's conference, a little too much fun, if you know what I mean. But don't worry I can be discrete. Given your propensity for secrets, I'm guessing they don't know you're a naiad either. Am I right?"

"How did you know?"

"I have a pretty commercial reputation, but I am a rabbit, a magical rabbit, but a natural being none the less with keen senses. I'm impressed by your ingenuity and your façade. I'm not surprised that you're having problems though. I imagine fairy work would be counterintuitive for a naiad. But that's neither here, nor there. What can I help you with today?"

"Well, I have case. A girl named Sheba in Tacoma, Washington."

"Oh, yes. I know her. Good kid. Very smart."

"I need you to give her ten dollars for Easter."

"Sorry, I don't typically deal in cash. I'm pretty sure she's programmed to receive the usual: spring clothes, candy, and a jump rope."

"But all that would cost way more than ten bucks. Can't you just give her the money?"

"It's not about cost, it's principle. I live by a philosophy related to holiday giving. I led a round table discussion at last year's conference entitled 'Clothes, Cash, or Candy? What Do Today's Children Want and What Should They Want?' I can dig up a copy of the notes if you're interested."

"That would be great, but in the meantime could you make an exception for this one kid?"

"Let's suppose for a minute I could, what's in it for me?"

The Naiad had not considered he might want something. "Is there something you want?"

"Do you know the average cottontail poops 300 times a day?"

"What?" She couldn't see where he was going with this.

"My worker bunnies are enchanted which helps manage things a bit, but do you have any idea what it means for my production schedule and sanitation expenses to be reliant on rabbit labor alone?"

"I can see how that's a problem, but I'm not sure where I come in..."

"I've looked into support services. I even approached the TEIC and the North Pole Eleven Alliance, but Santa and old 'Toothy have circled the wagons with iron clad non-compete clauses for all union members. The Switch Witch is sympathetic, but she's a one-woman operation with no workforce or power. The Leprechauns simply aren't interested. Cupids are free agents. I believe you have some at TEIC, yes?"

Yes, they did. Crystal had run into quite a few, even received training from one, a total letch.

"The bottom line is I've never been able to convince anyone to consider trading bunny labor for elf, fairy, or any other kind of workers. What I need is an alternative, some supernatural personnel from a market not yet cornered. Any ideas?"

"You want naiads to come work for you?"

"Do you think they'd be interested?"

She did. Actually the plan was brilliant, between global warming, dams, and pollution, this could be a new hope for her kind. She knew from her own experience that the change didn't come easy, but naiads could find meaning and purpose in brining joy to children. And they'd be working side by side with bunnies. Naiads had always had good relations with animals. The more she thought about it, the more excited she got.

Her mind raced with the possibilities until it stumbled on an unwelcome thought.

"EB, I'm under contract. I signed the non-compete."

"Well, luckily Priscilla owes me. I handled an ugly situation for her last year when the Cavity Creeps crashed the TEIC's hospitality suite during cocktail hour. What a wild night. The Creeps aren't such bad guys really. Fortunately, running a candy for breakfast holiday as I do, I have an established relationship with them and we were able to come to an understanding about how guests behave. It turned into the party of the conference. Those Cavity Creeps love their karaoke."

A few weeks into the transition things were going swimmingly. Thirteen fulltime naiads, four nymphs, and two satyrs joined the ranks and re-cruitment remained on the uptake. The ECC buzzed with new energy and ideas. Crystal loved her job and surprised herself with her creative management style. Even her long dormant love life perked up when Carl, one of the Cavity Creeps who came on as part of a demolition and construction pilot program, asked her out. He wasn't too bright, but he had a masculinity she found very appealing. Crystal felt truly happy for the first time in years. As she reflected on all this in her big, beautiful, cor-ner office with a water view, only a teeny tiny part of her worried that this was all too good to be true and it was only a matter of time before the other shoe dropped.

Her intercom chimed and her assistant an-nounced, "Bob from TEIC Social Media is here to see you. Should I show him in?"

Crystal's stomach clenched. She tried to as-sure herself today would not be that day as she stood to greet him.

"Bob."

"Crystal."

"How are you?"

"Good. But more importantly how are you? The whole holiday world is talking about what your doing here at the ECC. The reports are glow-ing. Is it as great as creatures are saying?"

"It's pretty awesome, but what brings you here Bob?"

"Well, there's something you need to see." Bob pulled an iPad mini out of his bag and flipped it on.

Crystal fought a wave of dejavu and tried to steady herself.

"Do you remember the child, Sheba? The one who started it all?"

Unable to speak, Crystal nodded.

"Well, she's back online and this time, she's gone totally viral. See for yourself."

The iPad displayed a simple water-themed web site with a large block of text. It read:

Share this post far and wide!

My name is Sheba. I am 9 years old and I have an important story to tell you. Not long ago I was obsessed with saving for an Xbox. When I was within just $10 of my goal the most extraordinary thing happened to me and it is something so special I need to share it with the world. I met someone, someone amazing who changed my life.

It turns out that there are far more important things in this world than Xboxes. There are rivers and waterways everywhere that need our help, so I took my entire Xbox savings, and with my BFF Meg, started an organization: New Aquatic Ideas And Directions.

We aim to reduce the effects of global warming, stop rivers from being dammed and diverted, and clean our precious waterways and we hope you will help us.

Support NAIAD today!

Naiad tears originate deep beneath the Earth. They are deceptively small for the emotional torrent they carry and Crystal's were flowing once again.

130.9

The Twenty-Seventh Try

Gabriel63 jerked involuntarily at the resounding wet crack. Nuts. He knew the sound all too well – toddler skull smashing into concrete – a thud, a crunch, and a weird sucking noise, followed by the child's piercing scream.

Technically Gabriel63 was not a he, but an it, genderless, like all angels, but long ago he had lived on Earth as a boy, so he still thought of himself that way. But at the moment he wasn't really thinking about that or even his injured ward because at the moment dread and dread alone filled Gabriel63's head. He failed again as a guardian and he knew he was up the proverbial creek – this sealed his spot on heavenly bowling league for sure.

Blood poured out of little Billy's head, puddling on the sidewalk. The kid wailed like the ambulance siren that would undoubtedly be arriving any minute, but Billy'd be okay. Gabriel63 had botched guarding enough times to know that for sure, but he, Gabriel63, on the other hand, was coming up gutter balls.

Moroni appeared with Gabriel63's replacement and spirited Gabriel63 away before the first responders got there.

Even with its arms crossed, its head shaking side to side, and its mouth in a quiet frown, Moroni looked benevolent. Moroni had always looked out for Gabriel63, taking him under its wing soon after the boy died tragically young, succumbing to mountain fever on a dangerous cross-country trek. Moroni had a big soft spot for Mormons.

Moroni had patiently mentored Gabriel63 through a long series of divine posts—choir, record keeping, messenger, harpist, scribe, and most recently guardian, but try as he might, Gabriel63 failed every time. Management would never let an angel with Gabriel63's track record near any of the more serious duties like destruction, security, transporting souls, or answering prayers. There was only one place left for Gabriel63 in the heavenly order and it was down, down as low as an angel could go, to the bowling team. Blessed Thunder Bowling was the absolute last stop for Seraphim, Cherubim, and Dominion washouts.

Billy had been Gabriel63's final, final chance to get it right. He wouldn't fight it. Moroni had literally done everything under heaven and Earth to help him. Gabriel63's head hung so low, his chin brushed his chest.

Gentle as ever, Moroni reached two fingers under Gabriel63's strong jawline, eased his face up, and looked deep into his eyes. Wham – peace and grace flooded through Gabriel63 and he was grateful.

"Despair not my child, I found you a loop-hole."

"But Billy was my eleventh infant ward. I thought that was the limit. Well, beyond the official limit, actually."

Moroni shook its head. "Even after all these years I see the human in you. It gives me great joy, Gabriel. Your heart is so true."

Gabriel63 wondered how this was possible, being the seed of two jack Mormons as he was, but Moroni should know, so Gabriel63 kept his counsel and counted his few blessings.

Maybe Moroni could read Gabriel63's mind, or maybe it was just so old and wise and loving that it intuited Gabriel63's thoughts, but either way Moroni cut right to the chase.

"You are not responsible for your parent's poor decisions young one, but Father knows, you have suffered for them."

It was true. Gabriel's pa Samuel gambled, drank, and generally ignored all the Prophets' words of wisdom. The family's wagon was devoid of hardtack or jerky, but so full of hooch, both it and Samuel sloshed all the way along the Pioneer Trail. Samuel's death by Indian arrow came as a huge relief to everyone except Gabriel and his mother Eliza. Young and pretty, Eliza rejected her brother-in-law's proposal as second wife, and found her way to a brothel somewhere around Wyoming where she lifted her skirt by way of audition and stuck around until cholera got her a few months later. All this left young Gabriel at the mercy of an angry uncle and his fellow Saints. A young boy from such wayward ancestry proved to be a burden on the whole traveling party. Little was spared for him, so it was only a matter of time before fever picked him off.

The Kingdoms of Glory are no place for a Latter Day Saint without family, so when Gabriel died, Moroni personally intervened, invoking an ancient and rarely used canon. Innocents who die can become angels. At sixteen Gabriel63 was much older than the typical angel candidate. But certain that young Gabriel would make an excellent angel, Moroni vouched for him. To date, Gabriel63 had failed at twenty-six celestial posts.

The stoop crept back into Gabriel63's shoulders and he blinked back tears as Moroni's angel whammy began to wear off.

"I bring good tidings, sweet Gabriel, the loophole of which I mentioned, it is your chance to at last succeed."

Gabriel63 looked up, daring to be hopeful.

"One thing I must prepare you for is that it is an adult."

"An adult?" Gabriel63 gushed. "But you always said we started with tots for a reason; all that cartilage and all. They bounce. They're resilient."

"Tarnish and discordance," Gabriel63 swore, "I mean, how many babies have I bumbled? I can't guard a full grown adult."

"You can safeguard this one, Gabriel. She's a loophole."

"What does loophole mean?"

"Well, in this case, it means, she fell through the cracks, a glitch in the system. She's from a wretchedly poor, underdeveloped part of Mexico and the registers down there are abysmal."

Moroni mused, "I've always wondered whether the poverty and misery resulted in poor record keeping, or whether the poor record keeping created the misery and poverty in the first place. It's sort of a chicken and egg thing, isn't it? It's the same the whole developing world over, so many souls going unaccounted for and caught in mortal coil."

It snapped out of its reverie a bit, "Well, that really is Metatron's department isn't it? Anyway, your new ward is Valencia. She is absolutely lovely.

She's twenty-two, recently converted to the Mormon Church, and married to Shawn, the missionary who converted her."

"It was the conversion that flagged the error and brought to our attention that she had never been assigned a guardian angel. A lucky break for everyone, not least of all you."

"It's perfect. A young, newly wed who recently moved to a much safer and healthier environment. She has a husband, newfound prosperity, and a large loving and welcoming extended family by marriage. What could possibly go wrong?" Moroni shone with delight.

As they located the couple's condo in an upscale neighborhood of downtown Salt Lake City, Gabriel63 felt dubious but hopeful.

"You've got this kid. I know it." Moroni dissipated.

Time to check in on the new charge.

Gabriel63 morphed through the front door in order to get a look around. The furniture gave off a genuine leather smell, confirming the sleek black living room set was no knockoff, but real top of the line goods. Every wall had been freshly painted a crisp white, and there were brightly colored accents everywhere—a red shelf, a green frame, a turquoise throw pillow, a yellow end table. The stark contrasts in the dark room made Gabriel63 think of one huge Day of the Dead sugar skull, somber with small expressions of joy. A cozy dinette set for four held an overflowing vase of yellow roses. The mantle displayed a series of black and white wedding photos in ornate matching silver frames. On the left, the bride and groom in traditional gown and tux taking the dance floor, on the right, a tiny flower girl and ring bearer holding hands, and in the center, an enormous photo of the groom's entire extended family in their wedding day finery, surrounding the bride and groom.

Gabriel63 nodded in approval and leaned in for a closer look at his ward. Small frame, luxurious hair, soft smile, she was lovely, as Moroni had promised. Everything seemed right here. His confidence bolstered, he decided to phase through the closed bedroom door for a real peek.

And there Gabriel63 found his new client, lying in bed, alone, her upper body propped up by pillows.

She was a vision, but a vision holding a small pearlescent handled pistol to her head.

Without thinking, Gabriel63 materialized and lunged at her, knocking the gun from her hand. It flipped backward mid-shot and punched a petite hole clear through the cherrywood bed board.

Gabriel63 found himself awkwardly crouched above Valencia with two knees and one hand on the bed and one arm extended. Both in shock, they gawked at each other for a moment until Valencia involuntarily made the sign of the cross, and action deeply imprinted on her in her youth, and seemingly appropriate to the occasion.

"Mormons don't make the sign of the cross."

"How do you know I'm Mormon? Who are you?"

It sunk in like a falling anvil, that she could see him, she could hear him, and he was headed to the heavenly lanes.

Gabriel63 untangled himself and floated to the side of the bed. "I'm sorry. I didn't mean to scare you. You're my ward. I mean, I'm your guardian angel. And you were trying to shoot yourself. You were trying to shoot yourself, right?"

Valencia looked down, but nodded.

"It's my job to protect you, although I didn't do it right. I broke at least a dozen regulations, but I wasn't ready for…what was happening."

"I never thought I had a guardian angel. No offence, but I felt pretty unguarded during my childhood."

"No, that's okay. You didn't have one then. There was a glitch in the system and I wasn't assigned to you until now. It has something to do with you being from a poor village."

"That figures."

Gabriel63 thought they were veering off topic. "Valencia, why do you have a gun? Where did you get it?"

Valencia shrugged. "It was an engagement gift from my mother-in-law. She says every American has the god given right to carry one and that every woman in a place like Salt Lake City needs one for her own protection."

"Well, now that I'm here, why don't we ease up on the gun for a while and try seeing if I can provide some protection?" As he spoke he picked up the pistol, set the safety, and placed it on the dresser. He spent a lot of time removing objects from harm's way with his previous toddler clients, so these actions came quite naturally to him.

"Valencia, why are you trying to hurt yourself? You're recently married. Recently baptized. Isn't everything ahead of you? Aren't you happy?"

Valencia started to cry. In little choking sobs she said, "Yes, I have been given much and I am grateful, but look around you. What's missing?"

Gabriel63 scanned the room for a clue. When he saw a framed photos of Shawn on the dresser it occurred to him. "Your husband?"

Valencia nodded and wailed, a surprisingly loud sound coming out of her small body.

"Where is he?"

"On...a...business...trip."

"That's not unusual, for a young professional is it? Do you think you might be over reacting a bit?"

"It's his monthly," Valencia made air quotes, "business trip...with his missionary companion." She let out big, air-gulping sobs.

"I'm not following."

"My husband is gay. Our marriage is a cover up."

Gabriel had not known anything about homosexuality during his human life, but his ninth baby ward had had two dads, bringing him up to speed on what it meant to be gay.

"Are you sure?"

"They take this business trip every fourth week, and there are so many late nights," more air quotes, "at the office. I don't think I'd mind so much if they were more discrete, but I think everyone knows and it's humiliating, humiliating and lonely."

The relief of finally having someone to unload on opened the floodgates wide and she kept talking.

"We've never had sex. Not once. Not even during our honeymoon. He planned it and everyday was chocked full of museums, and parties, and hikes, and binge eating. Every night we'd come back to the hotel exhausted and bloated. By the third night I knew it was intentional."

"Maybe I deserve it. When Shawn knocked on our door and asked us if we wanted to learn about the *Book of Mormon*, we said yes and asked him and his companion in as any polite family would. I was living with my sickly father and very old abuela. Shawn never judged us for our cement block walls or dirt floor. That impressed me. My abuela died about a month after Shawn first came to us. His kind counsel through my grief was our courtship. He brought both my father and me into the church and it was my father's dying wish that I marry Shawn and go with him to America to live a better life. I never really loved Shawn, I married him to honor my papa's last request, but I thought there would be sex, and children, and affection, and time to fall in love. I guess I got what I deserved."

"No, you didn't. Everyone deserves love and it's not too late for you. You just need a plan."

"What do you mean?"

"Well, what's important to you, besides marriage and children?"

"Shawn's family has been pushing me to go to college. My abuela always said I was very artistic, so I've been toying with the idea of graphic design."

Gabriel63 knew, thanks to the hipster parents, of his seventh, eighth, and tenth charges, what a hot field graphics were.

"That's it. You should go to college for graphic design. Focus on something for you. Make new friends and connections and when you're ready you should level with Shawn and tell him you need a real marriage. Shawn seems reasonable and his family seems loaded, I bet they could set up you with a decent alimony." Gabriel63 knew all about alimony, thanks to ward family number five.

"Shawn's family is well-off. His grandfather on his mother's side is from a famous singing family. Shawn calls him a 'lesser Osmond,' and his dad's side owns a local chain of very high-end jewelry stores. There's lots of money."

"Well, it's decided then. You'll go to school and study graphic design. When you're ready, you'll talk to Shawn and amicably move on with your life."

"Wow, you're really good at this."

"Good at what?'

"Guarding. I mean it's like praying, sort of. I told you my problems, my wants, and my needs. And you answered me with solutions. You're good at advice. You must have had a lot of practice, huh?"

"Actually no. All my wards before you were babies. They don't really have questions or prayers. Baby duty is mostly about prevention and removing choking hazards. Do you have any idea how many typical household items are the ideal size and shape to lodge in an airway?"

Having grown up in a household filled with less than a hundred possessions, Valencia couldn't really relate to this problem, but given his question, she assumed it was a lot.

"You're a very good guardian angel. Thank you. I'd say you pretty much worked everything out for me, except there's one more thing I really need."

"What's that?"

"No one here needs me. I thought I'd be supporting my husband and raising babies. I need to be needed."

Gabriel63 guessed he wasn't supposed to share this with a client, but he did anyway. "I need you. I really do."

"How so?"

"You are my last and final chance to get guarding right. If I don't, I'll be assigned to the heavenly bowling league. Permanently."

"Do you mean the game bowling? With the big balls?"

"During a heavy rainstorm, did your abuela ever tell you the thunder was the sound of angels bowling?"

Valencia smiled at the memory and nodded.

"It's true and it's where angels who mess up at everything else end up."

"But don't you like bowling? I mean, it's fun, right?"

"I guess I like bowling as much as anyone, but I do not want it to become my sole, soul purpose in life."

Valencia could understand that. "So, you really do need me, don't you?"

Gabriel63 nodded sincerely.

"You need me and I need you, so it's settled then."

Valencia closed her eyes, brought her hands together in front of her, and reverently bowed her head as a blurry memory from her catholic school days came back to her.

"Angel of God, my guardian dear, to whom God's love, commits me here, ever this day, be at my side, to light and guard, to rule and guide. Amen."

At that moment, the heavenly choirs sang, the archangels sighed in collective relief, the Blessed Thunder Bowlers raised their arms victoriously in X's, sign of the strike, Moroni beamed and sparkled like a disco ball, and the almighty Father grinned.

Gabriel63 succeeded.

It was an angel at last.

130.10

You All Leave

Lil pulled into the driveway and forced herself to smile. "Fake it 'til you make it," her life coach Barbara always said. Barbara intimidated the crap out of Lil, but Barbara, like most people, knew best or at least better than Lil, so Lil faked a smile.

As the plump, but pretty thirty-something year-old untangled her legs and skirt from the car seat, she looked around the yard for signs of the magic that she remembered. The once glorious garden plot was an overgrown mess. Just one brave zucchini plant and single stray tomato bush jutted out between the weeds trying to produce. A confused jumble of mismatched blooms and unwanted interlopers stuck out at all angles from Aunt Gladis's prized flowerbeds. Long faded strips of varnish flaked off carved Bavarian window shutters that used to give the house a cozy look. All traces of enchantment seemed to have drained away, leaving behind a cold lonely home just this side of derelict.

As Lil headed to the back door, still faking a smile, she reminded herself it would only be forty-five minutes and then she could leave. She and all the local cousins agreed to take turns visiting Uncle Gus after Aunt Gladis passed. Gladis and Gus had six children of their own, but they had long ago moved away. Far away.

Lil had always been the kindest of the cousins. She looked exactly as she was: sweet, warm, and soft. For the most part, Lil was the only one of her brothers, sisters, or cousins who actually showed up for her scheduled visits to make sure Gus was eating, keeping up with the house, and generally getting by. And because Lil didn't have a backbone, as much she hated it, she often ended up getting bullied into making other family member's visits as well.

Lil timed this visit before her Thursday Bunco group. This gave her a good excuse to keep the visit short and if the visit went sour as things tended to with Uncle Gus she might at least have fun at Bunco afterward.

As Lil tapped the sliding glass door she felt something crunch underfoot. She looked down and saw a row of tiny cups and platters fashioned out of leaves, twigs and little pieces of plastic. The makeshift dishes contained berries and water and other little bits of something. She leaned down for a closer look as the door slid open. Gus took one look at what Lil was looking at and shot out a slippered foot, scattering and destroying whatever it was.

"God damn fairy trash," Gus grumbled. "So you're here. Did you bring cookies, the ones with double stuff this time?"

Lil wanted to piece together what had just happened, but she was not one to ignore a direct question from anyone, so she looked up and nodded.

"Well, come in then." He gave another little kick and sent some of the strewn sticks and leaves skittering further across the patio.

Lil followed Gus toward the gloomy living room.

"What did you mean by fairy trash?"

"I mean god damn fairy trash. Those damn fairy farts leave their junk around trying to butter me up, get me to like 'em, but I know what they really are – nothing but pests. I wouldn't touch their crap if you paid me."

"There are fairies in your backyard?"

"The yard, the woods, what's left of the garden, all full of 'em. Your fool aunt encouraged the stupid buggers and now I'm left with a god damn infestation."

Lil wondered if Gus was cracking, but she had seen the little dishes herself. Was someone playing a trick? A joke? A smile and a blush spread across her bubble of a face revealing two deep dimples in her cheeks and one in her chin.

"Oh, you had me going there, Uncle Gus."

Gus scowled. "You don't believe me? You think I'm kidding? You never saw 'em Lil? All those times you played in the back with the kids. Maggie and Bridget never showed 'em to you? Not even Gladis? You never saw them once?"

Lil couldn't count the childhood hours spent in the backyard with her cousins. It was a big yard with a small wooded area behind, a kid's paradise. She did recall an inordinate number of fairy circles, the mushroom rings said to mark the locations where fairies danced. When they were little they talked about the fairies all the time and pretended they were there, but she had never actually seen one. It was just child's play.

"The whole back is filled with 'em. You wanna see one?"

"Do I want to see a fairy? Sure." Truthfully she did, but she thought he was nuts or maybe, hopefully, joking, no matter how strange the joke.

Gus shuffled over to his cluttered, ancient desk and jerked open the lower drawer. He pulled out a small box, walked back to Lil, now seated, and shoved it toward her.

It was a shadow box, the kind collectors use, with a hinged see-through lid. It reminded Lil of a butterfly box. Lil reached to take it and looked inside, but she did not understand what she was seeing. The box contained seven tiny people, each about the size of her thumb, each suspended above the backside of the box by a long silver pin through the middle.

Lil looked at Gus in disbelief. "These were alive and you killed them?"

"They're nothing but vermin. I trap 'em just like moles. After I trap 'em I put 'em in my box there. Pin 'em down and just let 'em go 'til they're gone."

Lil tasted bitter bile creeping up her throat. Uncle Gus had fairies in his yard and he was torturing them. He had always been mean. As kids, they had all been afraid of him, but this was way, way beyond belief.

Lil had to leave. She couldn't think straight or breathe. She fought the urge to full on barf. She tried to push the box back toward Gus, but couldn't control her hand. Her now iron grip shook like crazy. Then to Lil's complete undoing one of the fairies opened her eyes. The shaking must have roused it. In whatever part of her brain that was still operating on rational, Lil guessed this was the most recently captured. If Gus had filled the box as one might expect from top to bottom, left to right. She held a box of captured fairies and one of them was still alive.

She couldn't take her eyes off the semi-conscious fairy. It reminded Lil of the cherubic girls that used to be on toilet paper packages. Its pale, chubby face was surrounded by a mass of light brown ringlets. The peaks of two papery wings poked through the curls. The fairy's eyes rolled upward so only the whites were visible under the fluttering lids. She must be in agony.

Gus chuckled from his recliner. "Come on Lil, calm down, they're nothing more than flying turds. They deserve it. Trust me."

"Why do you hate them?'

"People are all the same, no matter the size. You just can't trust 'em. They act like they care, but I know. I know how they really are. How about a snack?"

That's how these visits usually went. After small talk Lil typically served up whatever she had brought and they'd split a grape pop.

"How about a snack?" Did he actually say that? This man was cruel and crazy. None of Barbara's life coaching tips prepared Lil for this. Faking it, for one, felt really out of the question. Lil's frantic brain groped at how she could possibly get herself and the fairy out of the house, and how she might help all the others in the backyard.

"Lil, cookies?"

"Sure, Uncle Gus. Just a sec."

Without letting go of the box, Lil turned and scooped up her purse and the plastic grocery bag she had brought with her. She stood and aimed herself toward the kitchen, still shaking so hard she barely made it.

Lil dropped the purse and bag on the counter and tried to control herself enough to lay the box down gently. She pulled back the lid and took one of the deep steadying breaths that Barbara had taught her.

As a kid, Lil had accepted a D in biology because touching frog guts was scary and confronting her science teacher was even scarier, but she knew she could not be squeamish now. This she had to do. She placed the pointer finger and thumb of one hand on the fairy's chest and legs and pinched the pin head with her other hand. Then she pushed down on the fairy while pulling up on the pin. Without thinking, she shut her eyes, but they popped back open when she heard a tiny faint shriek. Lil looked down and saw the fairy looking up.

Gus didn't say anything from the other room. Hopefully he hadn't heard.

Lil unscrewed the lid from a pop bottle and filled it with tap water. The fairy weakly took it and drank it straight down. After three more capfuls, the fairy poured the fourth over her pin wound. Then she just stared at Lil with helpless, soulful eyes.

"Are you hungry?"

The fairy nodded. All Lil had brought was Oreo cookies. The fairy seemed dubious, but broke off a little piece and nibbled at it. The fairy's puckered expression revealed an internal war between revulsion and hunger as she choked the crumb down.

Lil looked through the fridge to see what else she might offer. A jar of maraschino cherries seemed to be the closest thing to the natural kind of diet Lil guessed a fairy might have. It would have to do and fortunately it did. The fairy actually appeared to like it.

"Are you going to bring in those cookies, or what?" Gus hollered from the other room.

"Um, coming."

As Lil dumped the Oreos onto a plate an internal voice she didn't recognize, but that Barbara had been insisting was there for months, spoke up. Could she serve cookies to this monster like nothing had happened? Like he didn't have a troop of real-live fairies in his backyard, that he was systematically hunting down and murdering? No, this had to stop.

Lil placed a paper towel next to the fairy. "Do you trust me? Will you step on this towel so I can put you in my purse?"

The fairy stepped on without hesitation. Lil carefully wrapped her taco style and lowered her into the purse.

As a rule Lil avoided confrontation, but today she stormed up to her uncle and jammed the plate of the cookies into his surprised face. When he didn't reach out to take the plate, she let it drop in a messy pile on his lap.

"What is wrong with you? How can you be like this?" Lil demanded.

"There ain't a thing wrong with me, Missy. It's everyone else. You know what? Why don't you just leave? Get on outta here. That's what you all do, you all just leave…"

Lil couldn't bear to look at him another second, so she turned and left as Gus rambled on.

"Yep, just go on and leave too. Don't pretend you haven't wanted to since the moment you got here. Go on and just 'git. Leave me alone. That's what you all do anyway. Just go on and leave."

Lil walked out to the farthest reaches of wood beyond the backyard before she removed the fairy taco from her purse and carefully laid it on the ground. She signaled to the fairy to wait a moment as she scrawled on a sticky note. Then she got down on her hands and knees in an attempt to get her face close to the little fairy.

"You can't stay here. You and your folk have to leave. It is not safe here. Do you understand me?"

She showed the writing on the note to the fairy. "This is my address. Do you understand? It is a safe place. Not as nice as this, but I have a rock garden and a birdbath. You could be happy there, and no one will trap you or hurt you. Oh, I hope you understand. Please leave this place."

The fairy smiled, giggled, leaned forward, and kissed Lil on the chin. Then she tucked the sticky note under her arm and ran off, disappearing into her surroundings.

***

A week later when Lil didn't show, Gus hobbled around the backyard checking his traps. All were empty. As he picked the last one up he felt lonely and thought about his final hours with Gladis.

"You're going to have to be nicer when I'm gone, old man," she told him.

"I can't, old woman. When people leave me, it brings out the mean."

Gus stared into his trap and thought about it.

Then just to confirm what he already knew he went out to the biggest of the fairy rings, the one they discovered the day they bought the house, back when he and Gladis were young and in love, surrounded by their kids, and full of hope. Today, a solitary decaying toadstool was all that remained.

He had been right all along. He knew they were no good. He knew it was just a matter of time before they left him alone.

Just like everyone else.

130.11

Offending the Senses

"Maria, get out here. There are dolphins swimming around the boat."

She hadn't heard that excited, child-like tone from him in a long time. "Just a minute. I'm looking for my suit."

She was searching for her one-piece, because she just didn't have the body anymore for the bikini sitting on the top of the clothes heap that she had optimistically thrown in at the last minute.

"Forget the swimsuit and get out here," Ivan called. "This is a once in a lifetime thing. Let's just skinny dip with them before they're gone."

Maria felt torn. They had come on this trip to try to fix their marriage, rekindle the spark that seemed to have gone out, and what could be better for that than swimming naked with wild dolphins? On the other hand, she had really let herself go over the last couple of years and Ivan hadn't.

Maria and Ivan lived in Hollywood, a place where even the non-performers like Ivan who surrounded and supported the beautiful people needed to look the part. Ivan worked out for two hours every morning with a personal trainer before his long days as a soundtrack composer. Maria on the other hand, put on a good twenty pounds beyond the perfect size four of their wedding day some twenty years before. She worried that her poochy belly next to his sleek six-pack would undo the magical Mediterranean moment unfolding around them.

"Maria, they're amazing. I think I count eight of them. Come on, you don't want to miss this, and I don't want you to. We should be enjoying this together. You're my Puerto Rican water baby, so get out here and enjoy the oceano with me."

He's really trying she thought. The sex the night before had been okay, not great, but it was better than the long no sex streak they came here to break. She had to try too, so she swallowed hard and burst onto the deck bare-naked. She jumped into the water quick, concealing her all-too-prominent muffin top under the waves.

Encouraged, Ivan peeled the last of his clothes and dived in after her.

They splashed and frolicked with playful porpoises and each other.

It was more romantic than any candlelight dinner, bouquet of long stem roses, or gushy poem Maria could recall. They romped in the ocean together and made passionate love on the deck after.

Maria felt hopeful. Maybe they could find a way to repair their marriage, even with everything conspiring against it – the empty nest, for starters. Their one and only child recently moved halfway across the world to go to college. Ivan coped by throwing himself deeper into his work, and Maria turned to lattes and pastries, which led to weight gain, which led to self-loathing, which led to mood swings and outbursts that Ivan didn't know how to handle. But worst of all, the proverbial straw, was Cricket, a twenty-year-old, pseudo-rock star musician whom Ivan worked with frequently. Cricket relentlessly pursued Ivan. She sent him shirtless snap chat pictures, wrote love songs about him, and open-mouthed kissed him once in studio in front of fellow musicians. Even though Ivan repeatedly turned her down, he came clean to Maria that Cricket had hit on him and that he had been tempted. Maria went berserk, declared the marriage over, and went on a serious flan and rice pudding binge.

It took the combined forces of Ivan and a marriage counselor to convince her that they could work it out and that this trip would be a good start. Now, here they were, lying together, holding each other, and sharing pillow talk.

They reminisced about the past, the day they meet on La Posita Beach near her hometown San Juan, their first date at Pinky's, the night their beautiful Camila was born, but they also spoke of something they hadn't in so long – the future. He told her he thought his current project might earn him another Emmy, but this time with him as the lead composer. It was a dream project that excited him. She told him she felt ready for the kitchen remodel and new landscaping they had been putting off forever. She also divulged that their friend Sofia approached her about a part-time job that she wanted to accept, teaching Spanish to preschoolers. He said she'd be great at it. They discussed where they should go for their next getaway. Maria had forgotten how happy looking forward together made her. She snuggled closer to him and let herself remember everything she loved about him.

Maria snapped out of her reverie when, out of nowhere, the dolphins started whistling and breaching in a frenzy. Curious, Ivan and Maria got up and went to the rail to take a look. The dolphins swam in a circle counter to a swirling whirlpool that appeared out of nowhere. As the couple watched, a form rose up from the center of the vortex. A striking, pale-skinned, nude woman, with long, luxurious, golden hair ascended before them. There was no doubt she was Venus – she stunned them with her elegant, curvaceous looks, and stood on an enormous half-shell.

With a radiant smile, she floated toward Ivan and Maria and landed gracefully before them on the deck. Her hair continued to float around her head, though the air was still. "My dear, sweet, supplicants, you awoke me from a very long slumber."

Feeling very uncertain, despite the 'dear, sweet' part Maria decided to assume this was bad.

"Sorry." She offered with a puzzled shrug.

Venus laughed and it sounded like the most harmonious, beautiful music ever performed.

Something in the melodic laughter caused Cricket to spring into Maria's mind.

It was an awkward situation, the three of them standing naked on the bow of the boat. Maria glanced down and became even more uncomfortable when she saw that Ivan was tremendously, enormously aroused. Her eyes went wide, she blushed, and swallowed hard, looking away.

Ivan cupped his hands in front of his crotch in a lame attempt at modesty and blushed furiously.

Venus threw back her head and laughed even harder. "It's not your fault, Ivan. I am the Goddess of Love, the very embodiment of desire and sex. And it has recently come to my attention that you," she poked him on the chest, "are a very passionate man."

Ivan was at a complete loss for words, but Maria felt defensive and asked, "Have you been spying on us?"

In her serene, lyrical tone Venus answered, "Quite the opposite, my dear. I told you, the two of you awoke me from my slumber. A deep and long one at that."

"But what does that mean?" Maria asked.

"It means, sweet Maria, you have honored me. Your love and affection toward one another is the truest form of worship of me. You have produced such passion it attracted even my attention and I am here to reward you."

Maria thought she should be flattered, but this whole thing was just too weird and something about it made her suspicious. "What do you have in mind?"

"I'm going to make love to your husband."

Maria and Ivan responded in unison. "What?!"

Venus laughed her musical laugh again, but this time it definitely sounded tainted to Maria.

"Thanks, but no thanks, lady," Ivan said, but it came out far less forceful than he intended.

He cleared his throat and followed up with an equally half-hearted, "I think it's time for you to go."

"That's fine," Venus said. "I will give you time to clean and prepare yourself and for your anointment rituals. What do they call it these days? Deodorant and aftershave? Something like that? Get yourself ready for the greatest prize any man could receive, precious Ivan."

"But I don't want it."

"Yes, you do. I'll be back in three turns of the hourglass." And she became a mist that descended back into the sea.

Maria collapsed into Ivan. They both cried.

After a few minutes they wordlessly went below into the captain's cabin and dressed. They then moved into the galley and sat across from each other at the teak table holding hands.

"How can we stop this?" Maria sobbed.

"I don't think we can," Ivan answered. "I can feel her power over me."

Maria knew what he was talking about. She felt it too. Emotions overwhelmed her. She realized now her tubby tummy meant nothing, a stupid distraction from everything that mattered. Ivan didn't care. Their marriage had been solid all along, but now they had a real problem.

She burst out, "No! This cannot happen. There must be a way. I wish someone could help us...oh, I pray there is a way to stop this."

Ivan pulled Maria's hands up, causing them both to lean in closer. Through his tears he said, "Maria, I love you. I love us. I don't want this to happen, but I don't think we can stop it, but I do wonder if there might be a way to get Venus to stop it."

"What do you mean?"

"Well, what if we tried to make it unpleasant for her? Turn it into something she doesn't want?

Sex is a sensory experience. Is there a way we could offend her senses, perhaps?"

It was a tiny glimmer of hope, but it was all they had. With less than three hours, they got to work.

They decided Ivan would await Venus in the smaller, less pleasant stateroom with twin beds on either side.

When Venus appeared on deck in a see-through gauzy robe, hair still floating of its own accord, Maria, puffy-eyed and sullen just looked toward the stairs leading below. Venus dissipated and rematerialized in the correct quarters to find Ivan waiting and covered head to toe, in ridiculous, bright red, foul weather gear. His jacket covered bibbed pants that tucked into big rubber boots, and was zipped up as high as it would go. Ivan also had the hi-visibility yellow fluorescent hood pulled on over his head, so only his eyes and nose peeked out from his Gore-Tex armor.

"Cute." Venus waved her hand and the clothes obediently unzipped, unbuckled, and unsnapped, falling to the floor.

What was waiting beneath was worse.

Maria and Ivan covered every inch of Ivan with a mixture of grease, motor oil, and whatever other glop they found in the engine room.

Venus reached out and put her hand on Ivan's chest. The black goo felt sticky and slimy at the same time. The overall effect was like a thick layer of mucus tangled with chest hair. Venus pulled her hand back causing a sickening sucking sound, strands of the stuff oozed between her out-stretched hand and his torso, and globs of it seeped under her fingernails.

She flicked her hand unconsciously trying to shake some of it off.

She looked Ivan in the eyes, arched her eye-brows and said, "kinky."

Again, with a wave, the sludge was gone.

Venus looked slightly annoyed and Ivan hoped their schemes were getting to her, but she reestablished control of the moment by wrapping her hand and around the back of his head and pull-ing him in for a forceful, full-tongue, kiss.

Maria and Ivan had prepared for this too.

The revolting flavors of sardines, garlic, pickles, goat cheese, and coffee all mixed together assaulted Venus's taste buds. Maria and Ivan also drank more than a few consolation shots over the previous three hours, so essence of Tequila topped off the nasty taste.

Venus pulled away. Only her pride prevent-ed her from gagging. Angry fire smoldered in her eyes. This stunt hit the mark.

She opened her mouth to speak, but what-ever she planned to say was drowned completely out as Maria pushed play and the whiney crooning of Justin Bieber blasted through the portable Bose sound system Ivan never left home without.

It was the worst song in Maria and Ivan's combined collections. It only made it into Ivan's playlist because a friend of his worked on the arrangement and asked Ivan for professional feedback. Justin droned loudly about a selfish, unworthy lover. One so bad, even his momma didn't like her.

This one seemed to amuse Venus. To Ivan's annoyance when she waved her hand this time, she didn't turn the music off, just down.

"I love me some JB," Venus said, "he's so adorable."

"Ew." Ivan felt so much less flattered at being the object of her affection.

"You can't offend me with sound." She brushed his cheek with her finger. "The whole world sings praises to my name. The birds, the waves, music, even automated man-made sounds – all things audible exalt me."

"Okay then, bitch," Maria said from the engine room as she pulled a bandana over her nose and mouth and fired up backup motor number two.

The people at the marina who rented them the boat emphasized that backup motor number two was for extreme emergencies only. It was old and barely working. The insurance company insisted on redundant systems, so it was in the boat, but the rental company would not be responsible for any damage to ears, eyes, or lungs if it was used.

The low vibrating rumble of the machine was so loud it hurt like a jackhammer pounding through one's brain. But worse than the sound was the thick, oily, acrid smoke that stung the eyes, and flooded the nose, mouth, and throat.

This time, no amount of self-control could stop Venus from gagging. She doubled over coughing and choking before she had the presence of mind to kill the motor and clear the smoke.

When she stood up, her eyes burned with rage, her hair swirled around her head like flames, and her stature seemed larger and looming.

"Do you have anything else in your little bag of tricks? Surely, you must be running low."

"Maybe one or two more things," Maria answered through the paper-thin wall that separated the cabin from the head next door. She tugged at the cord they had jerry-rigged to release the atom bomb of mood killers, all the seals on the waste storage tank. It was connected to the toilet by a hose, but the tank itself happened to be directly below the twin bed closest to where Ivan and Venus stood.

The natural, skunky smell, something like cow pies mixed with rotting meat, was far more vile than the backup motor number two smoke.

Having learned from that episode, Venus dispatched of the tank contents swiftly, but not carefully; unfortunate for the dolphins, who took off in hurry.

"E-nough," she shouted. "This is an insult. You dare challenge me, the Goddess of Love like this? Do you know men would willingly die just to look at my face? That bloody, terrible wars have been waged in my name? I offer you this gift and you affront me? Who do you think you are?"

"A man who loves his wife. And his marriage."

"You are a insolent fool, and this has gone far enough."

With that, she pushed him onto the bed and straddled him.

But something went wrong. Their skin did not make contact. It was like there was a small invisible barrier between them.

From the back of Venus's throat a sound halfway between a moan and a scream of pure frustration emanated.

And then a third person joined them. They heard his low, masculine, merry chuckle before they saw him.

His appearance upon materializing was most impressive. He wore a bronze breastplate, tight leather breeches that laced up the sides, and gladiator sandals. His muscles bulged everywhere, at least three times the size of the biggest professional wrestler Ivan could picture. His hair was dark and wavy. He wore a meticulously trimmed beard and mustache and sported a wide, amused grin.

"Trouble, Sis?" he asked.

"Get the fuck out of here, Mars." Venus replied.

"Language. Wow, they really got to you, didn't they?"

"I don't know why you're here, but these are my subjects, so get out." She lunged at him in fury.

He caught her easily and turned her attack into an awkward embrace with her next to him and his arm hooked around her shoulder.

"Ivan, would you like some pants?" Mars snapped his fingers, clothing Ivan in a pair of swim trunks.

"Maria, care to join us?"

The door opened and Maria ran to Ivan's side. They stood close, arms around each other.

Mars turned to Venus.

"I know you think these are your supplicants, but it might interest you to know, they're mine too. They spent three hours petitioning me."

"We did?" Maria asked, grateful, but confused.

"Sure you did. You both wished and prayed for help, for intercession, as you prepared to battle a god. If that's not a shout out to the God of War, I don't know what is."

"You helped them?"

"Had to. They asked. And they made a damn good case. Frankly, they impressed the hell out of me. Either of them would make a fine general. They have solid strategy. Come on, Sissy, they attracted my attention, just like they did yours. How is it any different?"

"They worshiped me first."

"Well, you know what the new guy, Jesus, says about the first being last and the last being first. He's odd, but okay in my book—a pretty wise little dude."

Venus crossed her arms, stomped her foot like a spoiled child, and pouted.

"Marrrrsss!"

"Face it, princess, this skirmish is over."

Venus wasn't ready to concede, but Mars being the God of War knew a tactic for every adversary. Mars stopped smiling and respectfully turned to her.

"You know you won this one, right?"

"I did?"

"Absolutely. These two have a love strong and formidable enough to withstand the will of a god, not mention the most attractive and alluring god of all gods. That's all about you, Venus. It's homage to everything you are, reverence at the very deepest level for the power of love itself and that's you."

Venus knew she was being played, but this whole thing ceased being fun back around the blast from motor number two, and she wanted a way out.

"Okay, I guess you're right. Let's go."

She turned to Ivan and Maria.

"I'm going to let you keep your memories of this event."

Neither asked for this privilege, but at this point Maria understood Venus well enough to know that this strange parting shot made her feel in control, so Maria held her tongue about it.

The two gods exited in a fiery spectacle, and Maria and Ivan fell onto the little bed, both crying in exhausted relief.

But Venus was not content to leave it there.

They vexed her greatly, but it was nothing compared to how awestruck the couple left her. Their love was pure, heavy-duty adoration and Venus fed on it. It gave her amazing, new depths of power and strength. It was only fair she give them something in return – that had been the plan all along, so now in accordance with the couple's wishes she granted them the thing they wanted most.

As Venus exited the boat, she left behind a small, but white-hot ember – the very spark Maria and Ivan had come looking for.

130.12

Safe, Welcome, and Included

"I am pretty sure I'm the only paraplegic, black woman in the entire state of Idaho. So, you know what that makes me? Your faculty advisor. No one asked me if I wanted this post, they just assigned it to me, so here I am, and here you are. Welcome to the first meeting of the Magic Valley Community College Diversity Group for the academic year 2017-18."

Professor Goodwin pressed the joystick on her wheelchair this way and that, repositioning herself a little.

"This is southern Idaho people, so this is it. No Black Lives Matter, no LGBTQ alliance, no international students group, no nothing else. Just this, so go nuts."

She motored toward the hallway.

"Get to know each other and find ways to support one another."

"You're not staying?" Asked a girl wearing black lipstick.

"I have papers to grade. Sorry about meeting in a lobby. In my five years as advisor this group has never made it passed October, so if you do decide to keep going, let me know and I'll try to book a better space for next time. I'll check back in with you at nine, meanwhile this is your secure zone—you are all safe, welcome, and included. Respect each other and be respected."

"But, what should we do?"

"Introduce yourselves, talk about goals—guest speakers, lapel ribbons, bake sales, that kind of stuff." Over her shoulder she added, "and start thinking about officers, if you decide you want to keep going."

The five junior college students shifted around uncomfortably in functional black and silver furniture in the lobby of the fine arts building between the bathrooms and the counter that served as a ticket office. A large poster advertising the school's upcoming production of "Little Shop of Horrors" covered most of one wall.

A tall, shapely, Latino girl, caked in make-up cleared her throat and waved her hand. "I guess I'll go first. Life has made me the first to step up." She tossed her head to the side, swaying her loose brown curls away from her eyes. "No choice," she added in a murmur that seemed to be addressed mostly to herself.

Then to the group, "I'm Angel and I identify as trans female." She looked around for a reaction and then emphatically continued. "Yes, that means I am a female who was born male. And, yes, I do have a penis, but believe me it's small, and someday it will be gone." She waved her hand. "You know, twenty thousand dollars or so from now. Yes, I do take hormones, thus the boobies." She thrust her chest out a bit while making a circular motion with her hand.

"And though I am sick to death of answering all the probing and personal questions people feel it is perfectly okay to ask us trans girls, go ahead and ask me about the details and all the things you're dying to know. Somebody has to educate in this God-forsaken excuse for a state."

No one said a thing.

The black lipstick girl, sitting directly across from Angel finally broke the awkward silence.

"Cool. So, you're sort of like Sophia on 'Orange is the New Black.'"

"I'm sort of like the character Sophia? Well, let's see, other than the fact that she is a character, and her character is a criminal, in a prison, who is older than me, who works as a hairdresser, is married, and is black, and in real life is a rich celebrity with a huge following…yeah, I guess other than those things, we're sort of alike."

"I didn't mean…"

"Well, wait, we actually do have some things in common. You know how on the show she was jumped by thugs who thought they had a right to know what was between her legs? Yeah, that happened to me too. So yeah, I guess, like her, people think I'm a freak and I have no right to privacy."

With a flip of her curls, Angel decided to lighten up. "Oh, and we're both hot too. Am I right?"

It took the other girl a minute to collect herself. "Um, yeah, you are hot, I guess, and…brave. I, I respect you."

More silence.

Angel sighed and turned to her left toward a pasty, round-faced boy with acne and greasy bedhead. He wore a Boyance shirt that strained against his bulk and gazed toward the floor.

"I think you're up, lover," she said with a wink.

"Uh, I'm, uh, Norman," he said never looking up.

After another uneasy pause, Angel asked, "sooo, what brings you here, Norman?"

"Uh, my mom. I mean my mom thought it would be a good idea." His head bobbed up for a second. "She said it'd be a good way to make friends."

The black lipstick girl nodded encouragingly, but Norman looked back down before he could see her.

"She sent cookies." Norman rocked forward and back in little jerks and lifted a Tupperware a few inches off his lap. "They're no-bakes. We call 'em gopher guts in my family though." Norman followed up with a small self-conscious laugh.

"They're good anyway," he concluded with a shrug turning toward a pretty blond girl to his left and wishing with all his might she'd jump in for her turn.

Angel took the cue. "You're up blondie."

The blond girl emanated natural strength and beauty. Unlike Angel, she wore no makeup. Her hair was pulled into a simple ponytail, and she looked athletic and comfy in her pastel cotton clothes. She rubbed her shorts and looked around at each of them with her striking blue eyes. "Hi. I'm Randi and I identify as were."

Again there was silence.

After a beat, Angel probed, "what's were, sweetie?"

"Well, were, like werewolf."

Angel and the black lipstick girl broke into laughter. The other girl to the lipstick girl's left looked confused. Norman made screeching sounds with the metal feet of his chair as he tried to scoot it to the right, away from Randi. He had the most direct view of her freakishly long canine teeth. The chair would only move about a half inch at a time. After three or four loud scoots he gave up, but it leaned his whole body to the right.

"Are you for real?" Angel asked.

"Yeah. I am. I assure you though, you are all perfectly safe."

"You're a werewolf?" Angel asked. "As in, howling at the moon, fur covered body, running around on all fours, werewolf?"

"Yeah, well, only during a full moon."

"You win," Norman mumbled, chin still down, but eyes on her.

"Win what?"

"Win diversity. The lady said 'think about officers.' You win president. I mean you've got to be the most diverse here."

"Norman, she doesn't win president by being the most diverse," Angel scolded. "And anyways, what makes a once a month were-girl more diverse than and everyday Latino trans beauty?"

"Are you serious?" The last member of the group who had said nothing until now piped up in an unmistakable British accent.

"Okay," Angel interrupted, standing, hands out, and motioning both palms down toward the floor. She turned and pointed at Randi. "Let's put a pin in werewolf for a minute, because we are definitely coming back to that shit, Chica, but we haven't even meet the whole group yet." She sat back down and motioned across. "Lipstick, you're up."

Everyone turned to the girl who liked black. Her lips, thick eyeliner, hair, and fingernails all shined glossy and dark. A pleather corset hugged her torso outside of her shirt extenuating her large curves. The tops of her big pale boobs bubbled over the neckline of her low cut poet's blouse. She finished off the look with a full black skirt and combat boots.

"Hi all. People call me Raven." She nodded and looked around at each of the other members. "I'm basically here because, you know, it's hard growing up around here, when you're, you know, different."

"Different how, hon?" Angel asked.

"Well, you know, kinda Goth…I like different music, clothes, styles, just different."

"You're here because you're a Goth girl?"

"Well, I guess, yeah."

"Hmmm," Norman muttered. "Probably secretary at best."

Angel shot him a nasty look.

"Well, to be an ally too. Allies are super important, right? We all gotta be here for each other, right? Making sure everyone is safe, welcome, and included," she stammered as she turned red all over.

"O-kay." Angel turned to the last student. "So, what's your story head-scarf?"

"Please don't call me that."

"Well, you are wearing a scarf wrapped around your head, are you not?"

"We call it a hijab."

"Okay then, what's your story, hijab?"

"Jesus, show some respect," Randi cut in.

"Um, yeah, your not making her feel very safe or welcome, I don't think." Raven added.

"I'm Muslim. We wear the hijab out of modesty. It is part of my religion, my culture, and it is not okay to make light of it. My name is Feven. My family came here from Eritrea about six years ago as refugees."

A purple, lavender, and white streaked hijab concealed her hair, framed her face and draped in soft cowls below her neck. She also wore a long sleeve, silky, purple, blouse that belled out at the wrists and draped over a full-length purple skirt. Her skin and eyes were brown and stunning.

Norman looked back and forth between Feven and Angel. The other's could see his wheels spinning as he rocked and attempted to determine who ranked higher on his diversity scale.

"Maybe co-vice presidents?" he quibbled to himself.

"Your accent is really pretty," Raven said. "I don't think I've heard of Eritrea. Where is it exactly?"

"In Africa. It borders Ethiopia. I learned the Queen's English," Fever made air quotes, "from British missionaries in primary school."

"Well, hells bells, between a werewolf and a Muslim terrorist, I'm not sure who to be more afraid of."

All heads turned to Angel and everyone, except Norman, talked at once, but Randi was the loudest. "I told you, asshole, that you are safe from me, and you'll stay that way unless you make me decide different."

"What about you?" Angel asked Feven.

"I'm an American, and fully human, same as you. Muslim does not mean terrorist. I pose you no threat. I mean you no harm."

Angel decided to return to the were thing. "So, Team Jacob, you say we are all perfectly safe, and let me tell you I have a million baby cousins all around the Magic Valley that I care about, so how is it, exactly, that we're safe, if you are, as you say, a werewolf? Are the rest of your family werewolves too?"

"Yes. It runs in families, but of course, you can also become one by being bitten. And you're safe, because we have it under control."

"How many people are in your family?"

"Four in my immediate family. My mom, dad, brother and me, but we know other weres in the area."

"You know other werewolves? Do you hang out with vampires and witches too? Are you going to be bringing any imps to our meetings?"

"Do you really want to know?"

"So, how do you have it under control?"

"We just do, all right?"

Angel, looked around to the rest of the group and asked, "are you all okay with this? Are you buying the under control thing? Does anyone else here want to know how the local werewolves have their predatory tendencies under control?"

Before anyone could answer, Randi yelled, "we got training, okay? Cesar Millan trained us."

"Cesar Millan, the dog whisperer?" Raven asked.

"Yes, that Cesar Millan. My parents are rich. Most weres are. Being were has certain advantages. So my parents hired the very best to condition us to hunt chickens instead of people."

In Norman's mind, Randi sealed president.

"You were trained? Like a dog? By Cesar Millan?" Angel smiled.

Randi jumped up, lips curled, teeth exposed, and growled, "it was a solution to a problem, okay?"

"It's cool," Raven interjected. "You should be proud that you're unique, and that your family, you know, cares about people enough to, you know, try to not kill people. I want you to know that I respect that. I respect you."

"You respect that she basically part dog and hunts chickens?" Angel gibed.

Randi leaned forward, every muscle tensed as she locked eyes with Angel. "There have been one or two incidences, slip-ups, since the training. Wanna hear about them?"

Before he could answer, Raven cut in again. "She can't help that she was born into a family of weres, you know. She deserves our respect for making the best of a tough situation. Would you rather she hadn't got the training? What about all those baby cousins you are so worried about?"

After a strained moment, Angel responded with a shrug, tiny snort, and eye roll.

Randi relaxed her shoulders a bit and glanced back toward Raven. "Thanks, I guess."

She backed up and sat without taking her eyes off Angel.

Angel turned to Feven. "Okay, so teen wolf's cards are out on the table at least. What about you sugar? What's under that scarf of yours?"

"Hijab," Raven corrected.

Angel shot her a look and turned back to Feven, curls waving. "Sorry. Hijab. What are you hiding under that thing?"

"I'm not hiding anything."

"Really?"

Feven shifted. "Really."

"Well, then, take it off and show us."

Feven looked around at the others for support. They avoided eye contact.

Angel stared at Feven, while Randi looked toward the ceiling, and Raven and Norman both focused on the floor. Norman rocked. No one spoke.

Raven broke the silence. Without looking up, in a little voice, she said, " is it something embarrassing? Do they make you shave your head? Or mark you? Like, with a tattoo?" She sucked in a deep breath. "Or with a branding iron?"

Everyone looked at Feven.

"Are you kidding? It covers my head! There is hair underneath. What's wrong with you people?"

"I'm sorry," Raven blurted. "I'm your ally. It's okay. You don't have to show us anything. Sorry."

"She's right," Randi added. "You don't have to show us anything. Sorry."

Norman didn't say anything as he examined the hijab with suspicion.

Angel continued to push. "Well, I for one, need to know what's under there in order to feel safe."

"What do you think I could possibly be hiding?" Feven challenged.

"I don't know. Maybe a explosives, or a knife."

"A box cutter?" Norman offered.

"You think I carry a bomb, or knife, or box cutter, next to my head? Do really think that? Do you think my family came here to hurt people?" Feven's frustration turned to tears.

No one answered.

"Do you?" Feven shouted.

It was Randi who asked, "Why did you come here?"

Through deep sobs Feven replied, "Do any of you even know what it means to be a refugee?"

Feven looked Angel purposefully, straight in the eyes. "No one would ever choose this life if they had a choice."

She turned her accusing gaze on Raven. "You want to know something about Eritrea? The people there live in constant threat of war. They are arrested for no reason. You can't count on basic human rights."

She turned toward Randi. "My parents had to figure out a way to protect me. Military service is mandatory, so they gave up their high-paying professional jobs. My dad was a cartographer and my mom was a teacher, but they sacrificed everything to come here and work in a yogurt factory, so I wouldn't be forced to become a soldier or build roads. So I could be safe and go to school."

Her gaze moved to Norman. "So I could make some bloody friends. And I don't care how diverse you think that makes me. I don't want even want to be diverse and I don't want to be your stupid president or co-vice president."

To Angel, " I want to be accepted for who I am."

To Randi, " I want to people to understand I mean no harm."

To Raven, " I want some real frick'en allies."

Everyone sat in deep discomfort, stewing in the tension, guilt, and hypocrisy that permeated the room until Norman dropped forward out of his chair, and made his way on bent knees across to where Feven sat. Still looking down, he held out his Tupperware as an offering in front of him, "gopher gut?"

"Gopher gut?" Feven repeated in disbelief.

"It's something. I mean, it's a start, right?" Raven mumbled with a shrug.

Angel answered, "for the Magic Valley Community College Diversity Group, academic year 2017-18, I guess gopher guts are what we have to work with right now, so, yes, it's a start, but we've got a lot more shit to do."

Feven nodded, smiled a little, and took the offering.

"Thanks, Norman."

"You are welcome."

Resurrecting Rocky

In 1975 advertising executive Gary Dahl invented and marketed the Pet Rock. By the end of the same year he was a millionaire. He thought a rock made a perfect pet because a rock does not need to be fed, bathed, or groomed, and it cannot die, become sick, or be disobedient. He packaged the rocks with a care and training manual, one big gag filled with puns and jokes about tending to and teaching the rock. A clever guy gets rich off a simple idea – nice story.

But one has to wonder if Mr. Dahl was familiar with the concept of recognition – the act of bringing something wicked into being or causing a possession through attention, sometimes love. Recognition is the origin of spooks, spirits, and hauntings. Could Gary Dahl have known his funny rocks had the potential to become cursed items through the devotion of their owners? Could he have foreseen tragedy?

Probably not. For if history teaches us one thing, it is that the truest evil is born not of malice, but of ignorance.

***

"Mom, I found your pet rock in Grammie's attic. Can I keep it?"

Zoe plunked a cardboard carrier case, complete with air holes, labeled PET ROCK in funky 70's font on the table. It had been sealed with what looked to be several rolls of scotch tape, now a dried out flaky mess. DO NOT OPEN written in magic marker emblazoned all sides of the box.

"Oh my God. I had completely forgotten." Sarah flashed that smile people reserve for nostalgic moments.

"Your old care and training booklet is even in the box."

"That's right. I remember. I trained him to do all sorts of tricks."

"Grammie said I could have him, if you didn't mind."

"Sure, I don't mind. He's all yours."

What a stroke of luck. Zoe had been lobbying for a hamster or gerbil. For no reason Sarah could recall, she disliked pets, especially anything small and needy, maybe Zoe would bond with the rock enough to quell any more rodent requests for a while. That would be great.

Zoe loved the rock and named him Rocky, a predictable name, in fact, the same name her mother had christened the rock some forty years earlier. Both girls, all those years apart, knew without a doubt this was his true name because Rocky shared such information. Honesty and trust are the cornerstones of any truly meaningful relationship.

Sarah had adored Rocky, and Rocky had been devoted to Sarah, but Rocky suspected and hoped that maybe Zoe loved him even more. All signs indicated it. Zoe doted on Rocky. She made him a bed out of an old hand knitted scarf, she taught him tricks from the booklet, and gave him many caresses and kisses. During these times, when Zoe really concentrated on Rocky she learned things. He would do anything for her. He loved her. If she loved him back and loved him most, they would always be together.

All children instinctively understand recognition, and all adults spend years trying to forget it. Recognition causes spooks, spirits, and hauntings and it's hard, if not impossible, to be mature when you're afraid of porcelain dolls, looking into closets, and the ghosts floating around your house needing to exorcise old secrets, so grownups unlearn recognition in the early adult years. Recognition dwells in the hazy memories of childhood along with many other things best forgotten.

That's why Sarah was shocked when her brother turned completely red and choked on his coffee when she causally mentioned that Zoe had resurrected Rocky from the attic. Job slammed down his cup and shot up out of his chair. "That thing tried to kill me, Sarah!"

"What are you talking about?"

"Jesus, how could you forget?" Job paced in quick steps.

Job leaned toward her and whispered loudly through gritted teeth. "That thing pounded me in the face when I was sleeping. You swore up and down you had nothing to do with it. You said you weren't even in the room, so we knew it was the rock. Scott helped me seal it up and hide it in the attic. I wanted to bury it or take it to the dump, but I could never get the courage to retrieve it once we put it up there. I went to counseling. I still have nightmares! How could you let Zoe touch that thing?"

Sarah could tell Job wasn't lying but her memories were muddled.

"For Christ's sake, Sarah. You drove mom crazy until she bought the damn thing for you. You carried it everywhere, talked to it, and acted like it talked back. You kicked all your dolls out of your dollhouse, so Rocky could live there. It was creepy as hell even before the incident."

As Job spoke she thought hard and it started coming back, she had adored the rock and somehow knew the rock loved her as well. Their cousin Scott had come for the summer making Sarah the constant odd man out, so she shared all her little sister misery with Rocky. He was her confidant, her one true friend, the only one who would do anything for her.

Job remembered too and insisted they find Rocky and get rid of him, so they searched Zoe's room. They looked through piles of clothes and stuffed animals, inside the trophies on the shelf, and even hunted through the sock drawer, but Rocky was nowhere to be found.

"She must have taken him to school with her."

Job begged as he left, "promise me Sarah, you'll get rid of that thing."

When Zoe arrived home later that afternoon, Sarah asked if she had brought Rocky to school with her.

"No. He's in my room. He likes to sit on the window ledge and look outside. He especially wants to see when I'm coming back home."

Sarah could have sworn they'd checked the window, but no matter, now she knew where Zoe kept Rocky during the day and could locate and dispose of him tomorrow. Job had already texted three times asking if the rock was gone. Best to just put the whole thing behind them even if it meant they'd end up with a hamster.

Sarah slept fitfully that night. She couldn't remember her dreams well. They were vaguely familiar confusing flashes of creepy dolls that could move on their own, horrible things lurking under the bed, and apparitions begging her to listen, and through it all she felt an excruciating sense of loneliness and isolation. When she opened her eyes, before the alarm went off, Rocky was on the pillow not three inches from her face. When her brain caught up with her vision, Sarah suppressed a gasp and carefully slid her head back. She stared in disbelief at the smooth stone as she tried to gather her wits.

Rocky was going through his own, very different struggles. They had loved each other once. How could she even consider getting rid of him? Separating him from Zoe? Sealing him away again, so alone? He would have done anything for her. All those years ago, when she said her brother was stupid, that he was a bully, that she wished he would just die, he was the only one who listened. He tried too. He tried his best to do it for her, but he was young then; he didn't know how. He hadn't had all those years in the box to consider his haste, his mistake, to figure out the proper way to get the job done. He still loved Sarah, but he wasn't going back in a box.

Sarah rallied all her courage, quickly rolled over, jumped up, and dashed down the stairs in her nightgown.

She stopped at the bottom of the stairs to catch her breath and think. She'd get his box, put him in, tape it up and bury it or throw it in a lake. He's just a rock, she thought. Just a rock. What can he possibly do? Sarah sat heavy on the step.

The house resonated with the still and quiet of early morning, so even though it was a soft subtle sound, the gentle thud at the top of the stairs startled Sarah. She turned and watched in shock as Rocky thumped and rolled, thumped and rolled, thumped and rolled down each carpeted step until landed beside her.

The thought of her daughter sleeping upstairs flared in her mind. Maternal instinct trumped terror, so without real thought she grabbed Rocky tightly with both hands, extended her arms away from the rest of her body like one might hold a snake, and ran to the kitchen.

She plunked Rocky on the table. Her mind raced. Where was his box? She had no idea. She needed to calm down. Any box would do. She just needed to get a box and tape. Breathe. Think.

Somewhere in her scattered thoughts she remembered they kept boxes in the basement with the Christmas wrapping. And there was packing tape down there too. All she had to do was go down and get a box and the tape. She ordered her legs to move. She descended the stairs and rummaged around in a panic. In her desperation to grab the tape dispenser she bumped a mason jar filled with tacks and sent it crashing to the floor showering the ground with shards and pins. She'd deal with it later. Tape and box in hand she spun and attempted to pick her way through the piercing hazards. By the time she made it to the stairs both feet were bleeding and crying out for the removal of stinging slivers. She tried to ignore the pain and climb the steps.

Despite the agony in her feet, panic in her heart, and confusion in her brain, she almost made it to the top, but on the second step Rocky waited. He had considered this thoroughly during his many years in the box and calculated that this was the exact best spot for a misstep. He was correct.

As Sarah pressed all her weight down on her right foot some part of her realized it wasn't touching a painted wooden slat, but something much smoother and rounded. The rock shot out from under her taking her foot with it. Sarah fought for balance as her lower half flew behind her and she fell hard on her stomach knocking the air from her body. At the same time, her chin cracked hard on the wood and her teeth bit straight through her tongue sending blood oozing out the corners of her mouth. The momentum of the fall slid Sarah backward down the stairs, ribs cracking, shattered chin thudding on every single bloodstained step until she skidded to a slow stop at the bottom of the staircase, a gory breathless heap still clutching the box and tape roll.

It pained Rocky to see her like this, but she had lost her way. She forgot he was the perfect pet who did not need to be fed, bathed, or groomed, could not die, become sick, or be disobedient. The perfect pet deserved the devotion of the perfect owner, not to be alone in a box.

Under the Folds of a Homemade Flag

"Hi, Katydid."

Katherine wasn't surprised to see her dead grandfather. After all it's why she came. But after forty years it was a shock. Nobody had called her Katydid in ages, but of course, back when Grandpa died everyone did.

"Hi, Gramps."

She wasn't sure if she could hug him. He didn't seem substantial enough. He had never been much of a hugger anyway. Her second-grade self remembered him as gruff and their hugs as one-sided. He never shrugged her off; she cuddled like an eight-year-old and he more or less let her.

He appeared as she remembered him; broad shoulders, long arms, barrel chest, paunchy pear-shaped belly, drawn-out face with deep set eyes and high cheek bones, and scruffy silver hair with a little curl that swooped to the left. The only difference was that he seemed greyed out and pixelated, shadowy, but even so, his presence remained huge.

He didn't force conversation. Unlike most people he sat comfortable with silence.

Katherine wondered how much he knew. She thought a lot about what the dead knew, what they paid attention to, how checked in they were with the living.

"Sorry it's taken me so long to get here." Everyone in the family made the pilgrimage to Islay, Scotland sooner or later. Most sooner. Their family identity rested heavily on this cold, isolated place. It embarrassed Katherine that she had waited so long to come.

Her dad set the wheels in motion. Two weeks earlier a large manila envelope showed up in the mail. It contained a thick stack of papers and a handwritten note:

Dear Katherine –
This is part of the story of how you came to be. I
hope you find it interesting.
Love, Dad

She had. Katherine had always been fuzzy on the legend of her grandfather's heroic near-death experience in World War I, and this packet contained an account he himself penned of those events. She found it inconceivable that it had never been published, especially when so many of his lesser works had. It read like fiction, like a screenplay, not like something her grandfather, no matter how tough, could have actually endured.

It told the story of the 100th Aero Squadron, part of a contingent of twenty-three hundred troops, fledgling soldiers, twenty-year-old boys, some younger, embarking on their first assignment. Green as could be, they reported to the S.S. Tucania and shipped out for Europe, straight into an active battle zone.

The Tucania was torpedoed and sunk in the Irish Sea, between Ireland and Scotland. When Katherine told people it always struck her that it just didn't sound horrific, because Gramps' account described trauma wrapped in a nightmare.

The way he told it, at 6 p.m. they heard a crash on the starboard side. For the next three hours panicked men tried to make sane decisions. Untested soldiers struggled for some scrap of control in the chaos, but logic and order were going down with the ship. Scared and crazed, some just jumped in the water and died. At some point, the young GIs accepted it was every man for himself and yelled it at one another. Gramps miraculously made it on to the last lifeboat to leave the Tucania before she went under.

But fate plays cruel tricks. She spared him one sinking ship only to deliver him another, a smaller, overloaded lifeboat, in a freezing stormy sea, and it was filling with water. The darkness robbed him of all sight, adding to his misery, but perhaps it was also a benevolent shroud, sparing him the vision of shipmate's bodies bobbing in the sea. The waves were relentless. Their roar drowned out a hundred whispered prayers, but not the screams of the dying. The numbing wind made him dull and clumsy, but a man struck dumb has some small measure of fortune; he cannot smell, taste, or feel carnage no matter how closely it surrounds him.

Gramps himself wrote that it was only a matter of time before the inevitable happened, a conspiracy of wind and waves capsized the boat dumping sixty men into the sea. Then another cursed blessing as the waves slammed him onto deliverance, a small outcropping of jagged rocks that had so far withstood the unyielding aggression of the feral sea, but not without consequence. The age-old battle between earth and surf left razor-sharp edges in its wake, bloody handholds for an already bleeding man.

As Gramps fought to steady himself, the waves hurled a dark object next to him, another survivor. Gramps was spent and wounded, but this boy was worse. Gramps managed to find a small cave and drag them both slowly, painfully inside. They huddled together, soaked, freezing, and dazed.

A kind Scotch farmer found them this way in the morning and led them to his home. They trekked across the beach where friends lay broken and lifeless. The farmer and his wife fed them and made them tea.

Gramps and his comrade then joined a gruesome parade to the nearest village. Those who were merely wounded like Gramps took responsibility for the truly incapacitated, ministering to their needs and pushing them on wooden carts seven miles to Port Ellen. During the long slog, a count determined that fifty-four of the sixty men from Gramp's lifeboat had perished. The six still breathing were changed men, having experienced an entire lifetime's worth of anxiety, struggle, and reflection during the long night before. Valiant and fearful, heroic and mad, they had taken stock of everything, what mattered and what didn't. Character comes from being torpedoed, shipwrecked, and saved on the island of Islay.

Tears streamed down Katherine's face and Gramps seemed to know she was reflecting on his account.

"How did you survive it Gramps? It must have been so horrible."

"It was, Katydid, but not all of it. Some it of it was actually beautiful."

Katherine couldn't respond. She looked into his eyes trying to understand.

"Do you remember this title of my story?

"Under the Folds of a Homemade Flag."

"That's right. We suffered through real tragedy, surviving the very worst, but the story is really about that homemade flag and countless acts of kindness, compassion, and service."

"Those of us ill enough to be in intensive care under normal circumstances nursed those in critical condition. Believe me, one hundred and thirty-two injured and shell-shocked men taxed the resources of that island, but the villagers provided food, clothing, shelter, whatever comforts they could without question. Eighty-seven unexpected corpses were another terrible burden for the islanders to bear. As those kind locals prepared a mass funeral, they realized there was no American flag on the entire island. They knew our men deserved their colors, so the generous hearted women of Port Ellen raided their closets and sewing supplies to find the necessary red, white, and blue and they quickly and lovingly stitched the pieces together."

This was the part of the story Gramps dwelled on in his written account too; that the people of Islay handled this horrific unforeseen event with benevolence, grace, and dignity.

"It was a proud and beautiful ceremony, Katydid, under the folds of that homemade flag, made by the kindly hands of Scotch mothers to honor the sons of mothers they never even knew."

Tears streamed down Katherine's face. She had so much to ask him, so much on her mind, but she was afraid.

"Did you appear to the others?"

"No. Well, once, yes. But you're the first one who's come here to talk."

Katherine tried to wipe some of the wet off her face, but only succeeded in getting the backs of her hands slick with tears.

"Your dad, I didn't appear to him because I knew he had already started thinking about his own mortality and it would scare him. Your Uncle Bill, well, he and I said everything we needed to say while I was still alive. Your brother and cousins, they came here to honor me and for their own reasons, but not to talk, so I was here but didn't try to make myself known. I did appear to your grandmother though. I was being selfish. When she came here, she had five healthy, successful children, and nineteen loving grandkids. She had a lot to live for, so I materialized for just a minute to remind her she had something to die for too."

Gramps' vulnerability made Katherine feel a little braver. Her trip here was a mid-life crisis of sorts, nothing as flashy as a sports car, or as titillating as an affair. Dropping everything and flying off to Scotland was her own little freak-out, the embodiment of her big questions — What is it all about? Am I doing it right? Am I worthy?

She thought she had a pretty good life and was going about it in the right sort of way, but some part of her needed to know if Gramps thought so too, if he approved. She was proud of her career in education. While she had saved no lives, she tried to work toward the benefit of others. She adored her husband and cherished her daughter, but secretly worried, she might not deserve either of them.

After reading his account, Katherine saw Gramps as a man who had lived an entire lifetime of pain and growth in a single night and then had a regular life besides. Everything about the first life must have shaped him and made everything about the second life easier and more meaningful. He spent an entire night right on the line between living and dying, he saved at least one life while barely maintaining his own, and in the mist of all this, he saw not horror, but kindness around him. No doubt, raising a family, being a pillar of the community, even being Chief of Police, after his first life, well, it must have all been cake.

Dad's note said, "This is part of the story of how you came to be," but Katherine questioned it. Was she really somehow a part of all this?

Gramps answered her unasked question.

"Yes, Katydid, you are a part of this. It is your legacy. And your daughter's, she's beautiful and a spitfire. She's part of this too. Your husband, your cousins, their families, your brother, sisters, dad and mom and aunts and uncles, I did this for all of you and I'd do it again, you all made it worth it."

Katherine felt overwhelmed and relieved and sobbed harder than ever.

"I'm going to try and get your account published. Dad did too. I don't know why editors haven't been fighting for it ever since you wrote it. It's so amazing and important."

"Oh, Katydid, that's sweet, but it doesn't matter whether or not it gets published. I may not have known it at the time, but the story I wrote was for your dad, and uncles, and aunts, and you, and your cousins, and your kids. What matters is...that you know, everything I learned and experienced, it flows through all of you."

And there it was, the thing she'd been looking for without really knowing it – the point of it all – the honor, the wisdom and the growth. Like Gramps, Katherine would carry the story and meaning of the homemade flag into the rest of her life and try to live up to it. The ghost of Gramps had given her what she needed. Everything she needed. And more.

A Tempting Transaction

Sky Rothschild, the most exclusive real estate agent in New York City and arguably the world, wondered what this woman was doing in his office.

Working strictly by word of mouth, Sky didn't even have a web site for his business. He considered all marketing beneath him and accepted clients by referral only. She did not look anything like the kind of people he represented.

As the frumpy woman stood, leaned across the desk, and offered a hand, he smelled chocolate. In a German accent she said, "Mr. Rothschild, I'm Rosina Leckermaul. You will sell my house."

Seeing her standing made his impression of her worse. Sky found her remarkably unattractive. He estimated her to be on the backside of middle age. Her grey hair hung in a loose bob. She wore absolutely no makeup to conceal her unpleasant ashy face and had a growth on her nose any of his respectable clients would have removed in infancy.

She was clad in varying shades of black and grey. Her shapeless grey skirt hung over thick black tights and tattered boots with floppy laces. The large black buttons of the boxy cardigan she wore over a worn black turtleneck, were misaligned, causing the right side of the sweater to hang about three inches lower than the left. In stunning contrast to her drab attire, she wore an absurd hat. It looked something like a limp dinner plate, piled with fuzzy red pompoms, held on with a large bow tied under her chin.

Sky worked with his share of eccentric clients but had never seen anyone like her.

He liked the beautiful people, like himself, and she repulsed him. Being a practiced showman, he hid his revulsion with little effort and shook her hand. "Did you speak with my assistant Cheryl? She showed you in, yes?"

"You mean that Fräulein at your front desk? No. I shut that right down. I have no tolerance for being screened, especially not by kinder."

"Excuse me?"

Rosina did not reply.

"Please allow me to explain. I am a busy man, Ms. Leckermaul. It is not meant to be an imposition, but there are a few questions anyone needs to answer before arranging any actual face time with me. It is intended to save time, to make sure we are the right match, which I am afraid we may not be." Sky stood to indicate their meeting was over. "Thank you for your interest. Cheryl will provide you with a list of top-notch agents I personally recommend."

Rosina did not move. "You will sell my house Mr. Rothschild."

Sky started to say something else, but Rosina did not listen. She reached into her deep sweater pocket, took out a zip lock baggie, poured the powdery contents into her hand, sucked a big breath in and as she exhaled blew a grey puff toward Sky. "Sit down. We will talk."

Sky sat.

"May I ask how you found me Ms. Leckermaul? Who recommended my services?"

"My familiar, Blue Puter recommended you to me. And I found you the regular way, scrying."

"I'm sorry, scrying? Is it a business or family name?"

Rosina shot him a suspicious look. "Neither. It's using a crystal pendant to find what you're looking for…you know, divination?"

Clearly, he did not know, but Rosina changed the subject, anxious to get down to business. "My house is in Germany. I assume this is no problem for you?"

"Of course not, my clients are worldwide." As the words left his mouth, he wondered why he was allowing this interview to continue, but for some reason he kept talking. "Where in Germany, may I ask?"

"The Black Forest."

"That's interesting. Please tell me more."

"It is a special house, but modest. Around two thousand square feet. Four bedrooms. Two baths. The kitchen is an additional eight hundred square feet, but it is a separate building, connected to the rest by a hallway. It contains two industrial ovens. The lot is about five acres, with a half dozen pens behind the house."

"Once again, Ms. Leckermaul, I must apologize, but I only deal in properties in the hundred-million-dollar range. Exceptions are exceedingly rare…"

"My house will fetch your price."

"Really?"

"Ja."

"Do tell."

"For starters, although I've remodeled over the years and modernized inside, the house was built in 1315."

"Your house is seven hundred years old?"

"Ja, and it is made of confection and pastry," Rosina added with pride, smiling for the first time revealing crooked yellow teeth.

"What do you mean, confection and pastry?"

Rosina stretched her words a bit, as people sometimes do when they are thinking, "gingerbread, shortbread, stollen, streusel, marzipan, chocolate – and many gummies, kinder today love the gummies."

"Your house is seven-hundred-year-old candy house? Like in Hansel and Gretel?"

Rosina lit up. "You know Hansel and Gretel?"

"I know the story. Everyone knows the story."

"Everyone?"

"Sure. Parents tell it to their kids. It's a classic. Two kids find a gingerbread house in the woods and become prisoners of a wicked old witch who tries to eat them, but they outwit her and burn her up in her own oven."

Rosina nodded, her face melancholy. "Those two had gumption, not like today's fat, lazy kinder with their whining, and demands, and electronics."

"Are you telling me, you are the witch from the story?"

"I am."

"But Gretel pushed her in the oven and killed her."

Rosina cackled. "It takes more than embers and charcoal to kill a real witch, mein Liebling."

"Are you still in the business of capturing and eating little children?" Sky joked in an attempt to disarm this crazy lady sitting across from him.

"Ja. Eating, ja. Capturing, no. They come willingly."

"Children come willingly to your house to be eaten?"

"Ja. With their parents. I run it as an Airbnb. Eight hundred euros a night per bed."

"I suppose you eat the parents too?"

"Every once in a while, I'm tempted to, but just one night of that unbearable indigestion is enough to remind me how tough and grisly adults are. The kinder are best, but not today's kinder... they have no life, no spirit in them. They taste as bad as the adults sometimes." Rosina shook her head.

"You run it as an Airbnb? And people don't mind when you eat their children?"

"It is clearly spelled out in the contract, consumption of kinder may be rendered as partial payment." She tapped her finger on the arm of her chair in emphasis, as she said partial payment.

"Nobody reads contracts any more. Is this my fault? My contract is only a single page long and the cannibalism clause is bolded, highlighted, and requires initials. No one reads any more. They smell the streusel, watch their gleeful little piggy-kinder lick the shutters, and sign."

"Do you eat all the children who stay?"

"Look at me, Mr. Rothschild. How much do you think I can eat? One child, properly butchered can make a month's worth of meals."

"And there's no, Mr. Leckermaul?"

"Do you not see the red bollenhut?" She asked pointing to her crazy hat and shaking her head. "No, it's just me, except during coven gatherings. Now, my coven polishes off one or two kinder easily during festivals."

"You share the guests with your friends?"

"Of course, they are my coven. In fact, my friend Endora has been trying to convince me forever to go into business with her on a second guesthouse for witches. She thinks we could charge double, assuming meals would be included."

"Did you say eight hundred euros a night? That's over three hundred and fifty thousand dollars a year for the B and B you're running now?" Sky asked, doing all the calculations and conversions in his head.

"Kein, that's just for one bed, the house has six. I'm clearing one point five million euros a year now."

"You're bringing that in and could have a second house pulling in double? Why on Earth are you selling?"

"The fun is gone. The kinder are awful and their parents are stupid. There's no challenge, they don't need fattening, they never try to run away." Rosina's eyes narrowed and her nose and lips wrinkled, like she tasted something rotten.

"The freude is gone," she sighed. "I'm done with all of it. In fact, I'm going vegan. Blue Puter found me an app,' thirty days to a happy belly.'"

Sky leaned back in his thick Herman Miller Embody chair, his fingers intertwined except for his pointer fingers, which he pressed together and bounced on his lips. She had a nearly four million dollar a year enterprise on her hands. Sky thought of his last meeting with his accountant. Ira insisted that it was time to diversify. Business had gone exceptionally well since Sky left Christie's International two years ago and struck out on his own, but real estate is a volatile, risky venture. Ira stressed the need for a new, steady cash stream, it didn't have to be much, but it needed to be consistent.

Sky stood and offered his hand. "Ms. Leckermaul I'm quite glad you came to me with this opportunity. This is going to be a big win for both of us." They smiled as they shook hands.

"Oh, and that friend you mentioned? Endora? How might I get in touch with her?"

About the Author

Katrinka Mannelly writes and lives in Tacoma, Washington with her husband Brian, daughter Tigist, dog Apollo and cat Riptide. *Section 130* is Katrinka's first foray into fiction writing. For the past 23 years she has been scripting museum projects. She started developing content and writing for museums in 1994 and has since worked for over 30 museums, zoos and aquariums. Her writing has appeared in museums across the country including the Smithsonian, National Museum of Natural History, Washington, D.C. She has proudly contributed to the authoring of educational CD-ROMs and web sites.

Look for more books from Winged Hussar Publishing, LLC – E-books, paperbacks and Limited-Edition hardcovers.

The best in history, science fiction and fantasy at:
https://www. wingedhussarpublishing.com
or follow us on Facebook at:
Winged Hussar Publishing LLC
Or on twitter at:
WingHusPubLLC
For information and upcoming publications

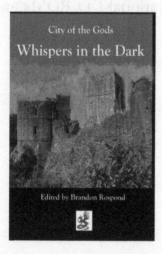

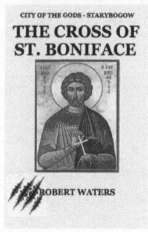